"I didn't want to appear vain," Miss Marple said, "but I couldn't help being just a teeny weeny bit pleased with myself, because, just by applying a little common sense, I believe I really did solve a problem that had baffled cleverer heads than mine. Though really I should have thought the whole thing was *obvious* from the beginning . . .

"A woman had been stabbed in her hotel room and her husband was under suspicion. But the situation boiled down to this—no one but the husband and the chambermaid had entered the victim's room.

"I inquired about the chambermaid . . ."

"The champion deceiver of our time."
                                    —NEW YORK TIMES

Berkley books by Agatha Christie

AGATHA CHRISTIE

THE REGATTA MYSTERY
and Other Stories

BERKLEY BOOKS, NEW YORK

This Berkley book contains the complete text
of the original hardcover edition. It has been
completely reset in a typeface designed for easy
reading, and was printed from new film.

THE REGATTA MYSTERY
AND OTHER STORIES

A Berkley Book / published by arrangement with
Dodd, Mead & Company

PRINTING HISTORY
Dodd, Mead edition published 1939
Dell edition / June 1976
Berkley edition / June 1984

ISBN: 0-425-06800-5

A BERKLEY BOOK TM® 757,375
Berkley Books are published by The Berkley Publishing Group,
200 Madison Avenue, New York, New York 10016.
The name ''BERKLEY'' and the stylized ''B'' with design
are trademarks belonging to Berkley Publishing Corporation.

PRINTED IN THE UNITED STATES OF AMERICA

Contents

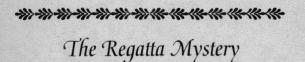

The Regatta Mystery

Mr. Isaac Pointz removed a cigar from his lips and said approvingly:

"Pretty little place."

Having thus set the seal of his approval upon Dartmouth harbor, he replaced the cigar and looked about him with the air of a man pleased with himself, his appearance, his surroundings and life generally.

As regards the first of these, Mr. Isaac Pointz was a man of fifty-eight, in good health and condition with perhaps a slight tendency to liver. He was not exactly stout, but comfortable-looking, and a yachting costume, which he wore at the moment, is not the most kindly of attires for a middle-aged man with a tendency to embonpoint. Mr. Pointz was very well turned out—correct to every crease and button—his dark and slightly

Oriental face beaming out under the peak of his yachting cap. As regards his surroundings, these may have been taken to mean his companions—his partner Mr. Leo Stein, Sir George and Lady Marroway, an American business acquaintance Mr. Samuel Leathern and his schoolgirl daughter Eve, Mrs. Rustington and Evan Llewellyn.

The party had just come ashore from Mr. Pointz' yacht—the *Merrimaid*. In the morning they had watched the yacht racing and they had now come ashore to join for a while in the fun of the fair—Coconut shies, Fat Ladies, the Human Spider and the Merry-go-round. It is hardly to be doubted that these delights were relished most by Eve Leathern. When Mr. Pointz finally suggested that it was time to adjourn to the Royal George for dinner hers was the only dissentient voice.

"Oh, Mr. Pointz—I did so want to have my fortune told by the Real Gypsy in the Caravan."

Mr. Pointz had doubts of the essential Realness of the Gypsy in question but he gave indulgent assent.

"Eve's just crazy about the fair," said her father apologetically. "But don't you pay any attention if you want to be getting along."

"Plenty of time," said Mr. Pointz benignantly. "Let the little lady enjoy herself. I'll take you on at darts, Leo."

"Twenty-five and over wins a prize," chanted the man in charge of the darts in a high nasal voice.

"Bet you a fiver my total score beats yours," said Pointz.

"Done," said Stein with alacrity.

The two men were soon whole-heartedly engaged in their battle.

Lady Marroway murmured to Evan Llewellyn:

"Eve is not the only child in the party."

Llewellyn smiled assent but somewhat absently.

He had been absent-minded all that day. Once or twice his answers had been wide of the point.

Pamela Marroway drew away from him and said to her husband:

"That young man has something on his mind."

Sir George murmured:

"Or someone?"

And his glance swept quickly over Janet Rustington.

Lady Marroway frowned a little. She was a tall woman exquisitely groomed. The scarlet of her fingernails was matched by the dark red coral studs in her ears. Her eyes were dark and watchful. Sir George affected a careless "hearty English gentleman" manner—but his bright blue eyes held the same watchful look as his wife's.

Isaac Pointz and Leo Stein were Hatton Garden diamond merchants. Sir George and Lady Marroway came from a different world—the world of Antibes and Juan les Pins—of golf at St. Jean-de-Luz—of bathing from the rocks at Madeira in the winter.

In outward seeming they were as the lilies that toiled not, neither did they spin. But perhaps this was not quite true. There are divers ways of toiling and also of spinning.

"Here's the kid back again," said Evan Llewellyn to Mrs. Rustington.

He was a dark young man—there was a faintly

hungry wolfish look about him which some women found attractive.

It was difficult to say whether Mrs. Rustington found him so. She did not wear her heart on her sleeve. She had married young—and the marriage had ended in disaster in less than a year. Since that time it was difficult to know what Janet Rustington thought of anyone or anything—her manner was always the same—charming but completely aloof.

Eve Leathern came dancing up to them, her lank fair hair bobbing excitedly. She was fifteen— an awkward child—but full of vitality.

"I'm going to be married by the time I'm seventeen," she exclaimed breathlessly. "To a very rich man and we're going to have six children and Tuesdays and Thursdays are my lucky days and I ought always to wear green or blue and an emerald is my lucky stone and—"

"Why, pet, I think we ought to be getting along," said her father.

Mr. Leathern was a tall, fair, dyspeptic-looking man with a somewhat mournful expression.

Mr. Pointz and Mr. Stein were turning away from the darts. Mr. Pointz was chuckling and Mr. Stein was looking somewhat rueful.

"It's all a matter of luck," he was saying.

Mr. Pointz slapped his pocket cheerfully.

"Took a fiver off you all right. Skill, my boy, skill. My old Dad was a first class dart player. Well, folks, let's be getting along. Had your fortune told, Eve? Did they tell you to beware of a dark man?"

"A dark woman," corrected Eve. "She's got a

cast in her eye and she'll be real mean to me if I give her a chance. And I'm to be married by the time I'm seventeen . . ."

She ran on happily as the party steered its way to the Royal George.

Dinner had been ordered beforehand by the forethought of Mr. Pointz and a bowing waiter led them upstairs and into a private room on the first floor. Here a round table was ready laid. The big bulging bow-window opened on the harbor square and was open. The noise of the fair came up to them, and the raucous squeal of three roundabouts each blaring a different tune.

"Best shut that if we're to hear ourselves speak," observed Mr. Pointz drily, and suited the action to the word.

They took their seats round the table and Mr. Pointz beamed affectionately at his guests. He felt he was doing them well and he liked to do people well. His eye rested on one after another. Lady Marroway—fine woman—not quite the goods, of course, he knew that—he was perfectly well aware that what he had called all his life the *crème de la crème* would have very little to do with the Marroways—but then the *crème de la crème* were supremely unaware of his own existence. Anyway, Lady Marroway was a damned smart-looking woman—and he didn't mind if she *did* rook him a bit at Bridge. Didn't enjoy it quite so much from Sir George. Fishy eye the fellow had. Brazenly on the make. But he wouldn't make too much out of Isaac Pointz. He'd see to that all right.

Old Leathern wasn't a bad fellow—longwinded, of course, like most Americans—fond of telling endless long stories. And he had that disconcerting habit of requiring precise information. What was the population of Dartmouth? In what year had the Naval College been built? And so on. Expected his host to be a kind of walking Baedeker. Eve was a nice cheery kid—he enjoyed chaffing her. Voice rather like a corncrake, but she had all her wits about her. A bright kid.

Young Llewellyn—he seemed a bit quiet. Looked as though he had something on his mind. Hard up, probably. These writing fellows usually were. Looked as though he might be keen on Janet Rustington. A nice woman—attractive and clever, too. But she didn't ram her writing down your throat. Highbrow sort of stuff she wrote but you'd never think it to hear her talk. And old Leo! *He* wasn't getting younger or thinner. And blissfully unaware that his partner was at that moment thinking precisely the same thing about him, Mr. Pointz corrected Mr. Leathern as to pilchards being connected with Devon and not Cornwall, and prepared to enjoy his dinner.

"Mr. Pointz," said Eve when plates of hot mackerel had been set before them and the waiters had left the room.

"Yes, young lady."

"Have you got that big diamond with you right now? The one you showed us last night and said you always took about with you?"

Mr. Pointz chuckled.

"That's right. My mascot, I call it. Yes, I've got it with me all right."

"I think that's awfully dangerous. Somebody

might get it away from you in the crowd at the fair.''

"Not they," said Mr. Pointz. "I'll take good care of that.''

"But they *might*," insisted Eve. "You've got gangsters in England as well as we have, haven't you?"

"They won't get the Morning Star," said Mr. Pointz. "To begin with it's in a special inner pocket. And anyway—old Pointz knows what he's about. Nobody's going to steal the Morning Star."

Eve laughed.

"Ugh-huh—bet I could steal it!"

"I bet you couldn't," Mr. Pointz twinkled back at her.

"Well, I bet I could. I was thinking about it last night in bed—after you'd handed it round the table for us all to look at. I thought of a real cute way to steal it."

"And what's that?"

Eve put her head on one side, her fair hair wagged excitedly. "I'm not telling you—now. What do you bet I couldn't?"

Memories of Mr. Pointz' youth rose in his mind.

"Half a dozen pairs of gloves," he said.

"Gloves," cried Eve disgustedly. "Who wears gloves?"

"Well—do you wear silk stockings?"

"Do I not? My best pair laddered this morning.''

"Very well, then. Half a dozen pairs of the finest silk stockings—"

"Oo-er," said Eve blissfully. "And what about you?"

"Well, I need a new tobacco pouch."

"Right. That's a deal. Not that you'll get your tobacco pouch. Now I'll tell you what you've got to do. You must hand it round like you did last night—"

She broke off as two waiters entered to remove the plates. When they were starting on the next course of chicken, Mr. Pointz said:

"Remember this, young woman, if this is to represent a real theft, I should send for the police and you'd be searched."

"That's quite O.K. by me. You needn't be quite so lifelike as to bring the police into it. But Lady Marroway or Mrs. Rustington can do all the searching you like."

"Well, that's that then," said Mr. Pointz. "What are you setting up to be? A first class jewel thief?"

"I might take to it as a career—if it really paid."

"If you got away with the Morning Star it would pay you. Even after recutting that stone would be worth over thirty thousand pounds."

"My!" said Eve, impressed. "What's that in dollars?"

Lady Marroway uttered an exclamation.

"And you carry such a stone about with you?" she said reproachfully. "Thirty thousand pounds." Her darkened eyelashes quivered.

Mrs. Rustington said softly: "It's a lot of money. . . . And then there's the fascination of the stone itself. . . . It's beautiful."

"Just a piece of carbon," said Evan Llewellyn.

"I've always understood it's the 'fence' that's the difficulty in jewel robberies," said Sir George. "He takes the lion's share—eh, what?"

"Come on," said Eve excitedly. "Let's start. Take the diamond out and say what you said last night."

Mr. Leathern said in his deep melancholy voice,

"I do apologize for my offspring. She gets kinder worked up—"

"That'll do, Pops," said Eve. "Now then, Mr. Pointz—"

Smiling, Mr. Pointz fumbled in an inner pocket. He drew something out. It lay on the palm of his hand, blinking in the light.

A diamond. . . .

Rather stiffly, Mr. Pointz repeated as far as he could remember his speech of the previous evening on the *Merrimaid*.

"Perhaps you ladies and gentlemen would like to have a look at this? It's an unusually beautiful stone. I call it the Morning Star and it's by way of being my mascot—goes about with me anywhere. Like to see it?"

He handed it to Lady Marroway, who took it, exclaimed at its beauty and passed it to Mr. Leathern who said, "Pretty good—yes, pretty good," in a somewhat artificial manner and in his turn passed it to Llewellyn.

The waiters coming in at that moment there was a slight hitch in the proceedings. When they had gone again, Evan said, "Very fine stone" and passed it to Leo Stein who did not trouble to make any comment but handed it quickly on to Eve.

"How perfectly lovely," cried Eve in a high affected voice.

"Oh!" She gave a cry of consternation as it slipped from her hand. "I've dropped it."

She pushed back her chair and got down to grope under the table. Sir George at her right, bent also. A glass got swept off the table in the confusion. Stein, Llewellyn and Mrs. Rustington all helped in the search. Finally Lady Marroway joined in.

Only Mr. Pointz took no part in the proceedings. He remained in his seat sipping his wine and smiling sardonically.

"Oh, dear," said Eve, still in her artificial manner. "How dreadful! Where *can* it have rolled to? I can't find it anywhere."

One by one the assistant searchers rose to their feet.

"It's disappeared all right, Pointz," said Sir George, smiling.

"Very nicely done," said Mr. Pointz, nodding approval. "You'd make a very good actress, Eve. Now the question is, have you hidden it somewhere or have you got it on you?"

"Search me," said Eve dramatically.

Mr. Pointz' eye sought out a large screen in the corner of the room.

He nodded towards it and then looked at Lady Marroway and Mrs. Rustington.

"If you ladies will be so good—"

"Why, certainly," said Lady Marroway, smiling.

The two women rose.

Lady Marroway said,

"Don't be afraid, Mr. Pointz. We'll vet her properly."

The three went behind the screen.

The room was hot. Evan Llewellyn flung open the window. A news vender was passing. Evan threw down a coin and the man threw up a paper.

Llewellyn unfolded it.

"Hungarian situation's none too good," he said.

"That the local rag?" asked Sir George. "There's a horse I'm interested in ought to have run at Haldon today—Natty Boy."

"Leo," said Mr. Pointz. "Lock the door. We don't want those damned waiters popping in and out till this business is over."

"Natty Boy won three to one," said Evan.

"Rotten odds," said Sir George.

"Mostly Regatta news," said Evan, glancing over the sheet.

The three young women came out from the screen.

"Not a sign of it," said Janet Rustington.

"You can take it from me she hasn't got it on her," said Lady Marroway.

Mr. Pointz thought he would be quite ready to take it from her. There was a grim tone in her voice and he felt no doubt that the search had been thorough.

"Say, Eve, you haven't swallowed it?" asked Mr. Leathern anxiously. "Because maybe that wouldn't be too good for you."

"I'd have seen her do that," said Leo Stein quietly. "I was watching her. She didn't put anything in her mouth."

"I couldn't swallow a great thing all points like that," said Eve. She put her hands on her hips and looked at Mr. Pointz. "What about it, big boy?" she asked.

"You stand over there where you are and don't move," said that gentleman.

Among them, the men stripped the table and turned it upside down. Mr. Pointz examined every inch of it. Then he transferred his attention to the chair on which Eve had been sitting and those on either side of her.

The thoroughness of the search left nothing to be desired. The other four men joined in and the women also. Eve Leathern stood by the wall near the screen and laughed with intense enjoyment.

Five minutes later Mr. Pointz rose with a slight groan from his knees and dusted his trousers sadly. His pristine freshness was somewhat impaired.

"Eve," he said. "I take off my hat to you. You're the finest thing in jewel thieves I've ever come across. What you've done with that stone beats me. As far as I can see it must be in the room as it isn't on you. I give you best."

"Are the stockings mine?" demanded Eve.

"They're yours, young lady."

"Eve, my child, where *can* you have hidden it?" demanded Mrs. Rustington curiously.

Eve pranced forward.

"I'll show you. You'll all be just mad with yourselves."

She went across to the side table where the things from the dinner table had been roughly stacked. She picked up her little black evening bag—

"Right under your eyes. Right . . ."

Her voice, gay and triumphant, trailed off suddenly.

"Oh," she said. "*Oh*. . . ."

"What's the matter, honey?" said her father.

Eve whispered: "It's gone . . . it's *gone*. . . ."

"What's all this?" asked Pointz, coming forward.

Eve turned to him impetuously.

"It was like this. This pochette of mine has a big paste stone in the middle of the clasp. It fell out last night and just when you were showing that diamond round I noticed that it was much the same size. And so I thought in the night what a good idea for a robbery it would be to wedge your diamond into the gap with a bit of plasticine. I felt sure nobody would ever spot it. That's what I did tonight. First I dropped it—then went down after it with the bag in my hand, stuck it into the gap with a bit of plasticine which I had handy, put my bag on the table and went on pretending to look for the diamond. I thought it would be like the Purloined Letter—you know—lying there in full view under all your noses—and just looking like a common bit of rhinestone. And it was a good plan —none of you *did* notice."

"I wonder," said Mr. Stein.

"What did you say?"

Mr. Pointz took the bag, looked at the empty hole with a fragment of plasticine still adhering to it and said slowly: "It may have fallen out. We'd better look again."

The search was repeated, but this time it was a curiously silent business. An atmosphere of tension pervaded the room.

Finally everyone in turn gave it up. They stood looking at each other.

"It's not in this room," said Stein.

"And nobody's left the room," said Sir George significantly.

There was a moment's pause. Eve burst into tears.

Her father patted her on the shoulder.

"There, there," he said awkwardly.

Sir George turned to Leo Stein.

"Mr. Stein," he said. "Just now you murmured something under your breath. When I asked you to repeat it, you said it was nothing. But as a matter of fact I heard what you said. Miss Eve had just said that none of us noticed the place where she had put the diamond. The words you murmured were: 'I wonder.' What we have to face is the probability that one person *did* notice—that that person is in this room now. I suggest that the only fair and honorable thing is for every one present to submit to a search. The diamond cannot have left the room."

When Sir George played the part of the old English gentleman, none could play it better. His voice rang with sincerity and indignation.

"Bit unpleasant, all this," said Mr. Pointz unhappily.

"It's all my fault," sobbed Eve. "I didn't mean—"

"Buck up, kiddo," said Mr. Stein kindly. "Nobody's blaming you."

Mr. Leathern said in his slow pedantic manner,

"Why, certainly, I think that Sir George's suggestion will meet with the fullest approval from all of us. It does from me."

"I agree," said Evan Llewellyn.

Mrs. Rustington looked at Lady Marroway who nodded a brief assent. The two of them went back behind the screen and the sobbing Eve accompanied them.

A waiter knocked on the door and was told to go away.

Five minutes later eight people looked at each other incredulously.

The Morning Star had vanished into space. . . .

Mr. Parker Pyne looked thoughtfully at the dark agitated face of the young man opposite him.

"Of course," he said. "You're Welsh, Mr. Llewellyn."

"What's that got to do with it?"

Mr. Parker Pyne waved a large, well-cared-for hand.

"Nothing at all, I admit. I am interested in the classification of emotional reactions as exemplified by certain racial types. That is all. Let us return to the consideration of your particular problem."

"I don't really know why I came to you," said Evan Llewellyn. His hands twitched nervously, and his dark face had a haggard look. He did not look at Mr. Parker Pyne and that gentleman's scrutiny seemed to make him uncomfortable. "I don't know why I came to you," he repeated. "But where the Hell *can* I go? And what the Hell can I *do?* It's the powerlessness of not being able to do anything at all that gets me. . . . I saw your advertisement and I remembered that a chap had once spoken of you and said that you got results. . . . And—well—I came! I suppose I was a fool. It's the sort of position nobody can do anything about.''

"Not at all," said Mr. Parker Pyne. "I am the proper person to come to. I am a specialist in unhappiness. This business has obviously caused you a good deal of pain. You are sure the facts are exactly as you have told me?''

"I don't think I've left out anything. Pointz brought out the diamond and passed it around— that wretched American child stuck it on her ridiculous bag and when we came to look at the bag, the diamond was gone. It wasn't on anyone —old Pointz himself even was searched—he suggested it himself—and I'll swear it was nowhere in that room! *And nobody left the room—*''

"No waiters, for instance?" suggested Mr. Parker Pyne.

Llewellyn shook his head.

"They went out before the girl began messing about with the diamond, and afterwards Pointz locked the door so as to keep them out. No, it lies between one of us.''

"It would certainly seem so," said Mr. Parker Pyne thoughtfully.

"That damned evening paper," said Evan Lewellyn bitterly. "I saw it come into their minds— that that was the only way—''

"Just tell me again exactly what occurred."

"It was perfectly simple. I threw open the window, whistled to the man, threw down a copper and he tossed me up the paper. And there it is, you see—the only possible way the diamond could have left the room—thrown by me to an accomplice waiting in the street below."

"Not the *only* possible way," said Mr. Parker Pyne.

"What other way can you suggest?"

"If you didn't throw it out, there *must* have been some other way."

"Oh, I see. I hoped you meant something more definite than that. Well, I can only say that I *didn't* throw it out. I can't expect you to believe me—or anyone else."

"Oh, yes, I believe you," said Mr. Parker Pyne.

"You do? Why?"

"Not a criminal type," said Mr. Parker Pyne. "Not, that is, the particular criminal type that steals jewelry. There are crimes, of course, that you might commit—but we won't enter into that subject. At any rate I do not see you as the purloiner of the Morning Star."

"Everyone else does though," said Llewellyn bitterly.

"I see," said Mr. Parker Pyne.

"They looked at me in a queer sort of way at the time. Marroway picked up the paper and just glanced over at the window. He didn't say anything. But Pointz cottoned on to it quick enough! I could see what they thought. There hasn't been any open accusation, that's the devil of it."

Mr. Parker Pyne nodded sympathetically.

"It is worse than that," he said.

"Yes. It's just suspicion. I've had a fellow

round asking questions—routine inquiries, he called it. One of the new dress-shirted lot of police, I suppose. Very tactful—nothing at all hinted. Just interested in the fact that I'd been hard up and was suddenly cutting a bit of a splash.''

"And were you?"

"Yes—some luck with a horse or two. Unluckily my bets were made on the course—there's nothing to show that that's how the money came in. They can't disprove it, of course—but that's just the sort of easy lie a fellow would invent if he didn't want to show where the money came from.''

"I agree. Still they will have to have a good deal more than that to go upon."

"Oh! I'm not afraid of actually being arrested and charged with the theft. In a way that would be easier—one would know where one was. It's the ghastly fact that all those people believe I took it.''

"One person in particular?"

"What do you mean?"

"A suggestion—nothing more—" Again Mr. Parker Pyne waved his comfortable-looking hand. "There *was* one person in particular, wasn't there? Shall we say Mrs. Rustington?"

Llewellyn's dark face flushed.

"Why pitch on her?"

"Oh, my dear sir—there is obviously someone whose opinion matters to you greatly—probably a lady. What ladies were there? An American flapper? Lady Marroway? But you would probably rise not fall in Lady Marroway's estimation if you had brought off such a coup. I know something of the lady. Clearly then, Mrs. Rustington.''

Llewellyn said with something of an effort,

''She—she's had rather an unfortunate experience. Her husband was a down and out rotter. It's made her unwilling to trust anyone. She—if she thinks—''

He found it difficult to go on.

''Quite so,'' said Mr. Parker Pyne. ''I see the matter is important. It must be cleared up.''

Evan gave a short laugh.

''That's easy to say.''

''And quite easy to do,'' said Mr. Parker Pyne.

''You think so?''

''Oh, yes—the problem is so clear cut. So many possibilities are ruled out. The answer must really be extremely simple. Indeed already I have a kind of glimmering—''

Llewellyn stared at him incredulously.

Mr. Parker Pyne drew a pad of paper towards him and picked up a pen.

''Perhaps you would give me a brief description of the party.''

''Haven't I already done so?''

''Their personal appearance—color of hair and so on.''

''But, Mr. Parker Pyne, what can that have to do with it?''

''A good deal, young man, a good deal. Classification and so on.''

Somewhat unbelievingly, Evan described the personal appearance of the members of the yachting party.

Mr. Parker Pyne made a note or two, pushed away the pad and said:

"Excellent. By the way, did you say a wine-glass was broken?"

Evan stared again.

"Yes, it was knocked off the table and then it got stepped on."

"Nasty thing, splinters of glass," said Mr. Parker Pyne. "Whose wine-glass was it?"

"I think it was the child's—Eve."

"Ah!—and who sat next to her on that side?"

"Sir George Marroway."

"You didn't see which of them knocked it off the table?"

"Afraid I didn't. Does it matter?"

"Not really. No. That was a superfluous question. Well"—he stood up—"good morning, Mr. Llewellyn. Will you call again in three days' time? I think the whole thing will be quite satisfactorily cleared up by then."

"Are you joking, Mr. Parker Pyne?"

"I never joke on professional matters, my dear sir. It would occasion distrust in my clients. Shall we say Friday at 11:30? Thank you."

Evan entered Mr. Parker Pyne's office on the Friday morning in a considerable turmoil. Hope and skepticism fought for mastery.

Mr. Parker Pyne rose to meet him with a beaming smile.

"Good morning, Mr. Llewellyn. Sit down. Have a cigarette?"

Llewellyn waved aside the proffered box.

"Well?" he said.

"Very well indeed," said Mr. Parker Pyne. "The police arrested the gang last night."

"The gang? What gang?"

"The Amalfi gang. I thought of them at once when you told me your story. I recognized their methods and once you had described the guests, well, there was no doubt at all in my mind."

"Who are the Amalfi gang?"

"Father, son and daughter-in-law—that is if Pietro and Maria are really married—which some doubt."

"I don't understand."

"It's quite simple. The name is Italian and no doubt the origin is Italian, but old Amalfi was born in America. His methods are usually the same. He impersonates a real business man, introduces himself to some prominent figure in the jewel business in some European country and then plays his little trick. In this case he was deliberately on the track of the Morning Star. Pointz' idiosyncrasy was well known in the trade. Maria Amalfi played the part of his daughter (amazing creature, twenty-seven at least, and nearly always plays a part of sixteen)."

"Not Eve!" gasped Llewellyn.

"Exactly. The third member of the gang got himself taken on as an extra waiter at the Royal George—it was holiday time, remember, and they would need extra staff. He may even have bribed a regular man to stay away. The scene is set. Eve challenges old Pointz and he takes on the bet. He passes round the diamond as he had done the night before. The waiters enter the room and Leathern retains the stone until they have left the room. When they do leave, the diamond leaves also, neatly attached with a morsel of chewing gum to the underside of the plate that Pietro bears away. So simple!''

''But I *saw* it after that.''

''No, no, you saw a paste replica, good enough to deceive a casual glance. Stein, you told me, hardly looked at it. Eve drops it, sweeps off a glass too and steps firmly on stone and glass together. Miraculous disappearance of diamond. Both Eve and Leathern can submit to as much searching as anyone pleases.''

''Well—I'm—'' Evan shook his head, at a loss for words.

''You say you recognized the gang from my description. Had they worked this trick before?''

''Not exactly—but it was their kind of business. Naturally my attention was at once directed to the girl Eve.''

''Why? I didn't suspect her—nobody did. She seemed such a—such a *child*.''

''That is the peculiar genius of Maria Amalfi. She is more like a child than any child could possibly be! And then the plasticine! This bet was supposed to have arisen quite spontaneously—yet the little lady had some plasticine with her all handy. That spoke of premeditation. My suspicions fastened on her at once.''

Llewellyn rose to his feet.

''Well, Mr. Parker Pyne, I'm no end obliged to you.''

''Classification,'' murmured Mr. Parker Pyne. ''The classification of criminal types—it interests me.''

''You'll let me know how much—er—''

''My fee will be quite moderate,'' said Mr.

Parker Pyne. "It will not make too big a hole in the—er—horse racing profits. All the same, young man, I should, I think, leave the horses alone in future. Very uncertain animal, the horse."

"That's all right," said Evan.

He shook Mr. Parker Pyne by the hand and strode from the office.

He hailed a taxi and gave the address of Janet Rustington's flat.

He felt in a mood to carry all before him.

The Mystery
of the Bagdad Chest

The words made a catchy headline, and I said as much to my friend, Hercule Poirot. I knew none of the parties. My interest was merely the dispassionate one of the man in the street. Poirot agreed.

"Yes, it has a flavor of the Oriental, of the mysterious. The chest may very well have been a sham Jacobean one from the Tottenham Court Road; none the less the reporter who thought of naming it the Bagdad Chest was happily inspired. The word 'Mystery' is also thoughtfully placed in juxtaposition, though I understand there is very little mystery about the case."

"Exactly. It is all rather horrible and macabre, but it is not mysterious."

"Horrible and macabre," repeated Poirot thoughtfully.

"The whole idea is revolting," I said, rising to

29

my feet and pacing up and down the room. "The murderer kills this man—his friend—shoves him into the chest, and half an hour later is dancing in that same room with the wife of his victim. Think! If she had imagined for one moment—"

"True," said Poirot thoughtfully. "That much-vaunted possession, a woman's intuition—it does not seem to have been working."

"The party seems to have gone off very merrily," I said with a slight shiver. "And all that time, as they danced and played poker, there was a dead man in the room with them. One could write a play about such an idea."

"It has been done," said Poirot. "But console yourself, Hastings," he added kindly. "Because a theme has been used once, there is no reason why it should not be used again. Compose your drama."

I had picked up the paper and was studying the rather blurred reproduction of a photograph.

"She must be a beautiful woman," I said slowly. "Even from this, one gets an idea."

Below the picture ran the inscription:

A RECENT PORTRAIT OF MRS. CLAYTON, THE WIFE OF THE MURDERED MAN

Poirot took the paper from me.

"Yes," he said. "She is beautiful. Doubtless she is of those born to trouble the souls of men."

He handed the paper back to me with a sigh.

"*Dieu merci*, I am not of an ardent temperament. It has saved me from many embarrassments. I am duly thankful."

I do not remember that we discussed the case further. Poirot displayed no special interest in it at the time. The facts were so clear, and there was so little ambiguity about them, that discussion seemed merely futile.

Mr. and Mrs. Clayton and Major Rich were friends of fairly long standing. On the day in question, the tenth of March, the Claytons had accepted an invitation to spend the evening with Major Rich. At about seven-thirty, however, Clayton explained to another friend, a Major Curtiss, with whom he was having a drink, that he had been unexpectedly called to Scotland and was leaving by the eight o'clock train.

"I'll just have time to drop in and explain to old Jack," went on Clayton. "Marguerita is going, of course. I'm sorry about it, but Jack will understand how it is."

Mr. Clayton was as good as his word. He arrived at Major Rich's rooms about twenty to eight. The major was out at the time, but his manservant, who knew Mr. Clayton well, suggested that he come in and wait. Mr. Clayton said that he had not time, but that he would come in and write a note. He added that he was on his way to catch a train.

The valet accordingly showed him into the sitting room.

About five minutes later Major Rich, who must have let himself in without the valet hearing him, opened the door of the sitting room, called his man and told him to go out and get some cigarettes. On his return the man brought them to his master, who was then alone in the sitting room.

The man naturally concluded that Mr. Clayton had left.

The guests arrived shortly afterwards. They comprised Mrs. Clayton, Major Curtiss and a Mr. and Mrs. Spence. The evening was spent dancing to the phonograph and playing poker. The guests left shortly after midnight.

The following morning, on coming to do the sitting room, the valet was startled to find a deep stain discoloring the carpet below and in front of a piece of furniture which Major Rich had brought from the East and which was called the Bagdad Chest.

Instinctively the valet lifted the lid of the chest and was horrified to find inside the doubled-up body of a man who had been stabbed to the heart.

Terrified, the man ran out of the flat and fetched the nearest policeman. The dead man proved to be Mr. Clayton. The arrest of Major Rich followed very shortly afterward. The major's defense, it was understood, consisted of a sturdy denial of everything. He had not seen Mr. Clayton the preceding evening and the first he had heard of his going to Scotland had been from Mrs. Clayton.

Such were the bald facts of the case. Innuendoes and suggestions naturally abounded. The close friendship and intimacy of Major Rich and Mrs. Clayton were so stressed that only a fool could fail to read between the lines. The motive for the crime was plainly indicated.

Long experience has taught me to make allowance for baseless calumny. The motive suggested might, for all the evidence, be entirely nonexis-

tent. Some quite other reason might have precipi-
tated the issue. But one thing did stand out clearly
—that Rich was the murderer.

As I say, the matter might have rested there,
had it not happened that Poirot and I were due at
a party given by Lady Chatterton that night.

Poirot, whilst bemoaning social engagements
and declaring a passion for solitude, really enjoyed these affairs enormously. To be made a fuss
of and treated as a lion suited him down to the
ground.

On occasions he positively purred! I have seen
him blandly receiving the most outrageous compliments as no more than his due, and uttering the
most blatantly conceited remarks, such as I can
hardly bear to set down.

Sometimes he would argue with me on the subject.

"But, my friend, I am not an Anglo-Saxon.
Why should I play the hypocrite? *Si, si,* that is
what you do, all of you. The airman who has
made a difficult flight, the tennis champion—they
look down their noses, they mutter inaudibly that
'it is nothing.' But do they really think that themselves? Not for a moment. They would admire the
exploit in someone else. So, being reasonable men,
they admire it in themselves. But their training
prevents them from saying so. Me, I am not like
that. The talents that I possess—I would salute
them in another. As it happens, in my own particular line, there is no one to touch me. *C'est dom-
mage!* As it is, I admit freely and without the hy-
pocrisy that I am a great man. I have the order,
the method and the psychology in an unusual de-

gree. I am, in fact, Hercule Poirot! Why should I turn red and stammer and mutter into my chin that really I am very stupid? It would not be true.''

"There is certainly only one Hercule Poirot," I agreed—not without a spice of malice, of which, fortunately, Poirot remained quite oblivious.

Lady Chatterton was one of Poirot's most ardent admirers. Starting from the mysterious conduct of a Pekingese, he had unraveled a chain which led to a noted burglar and housebreaker. Lady Chatterton had been loud in his praises ever since.

To see Poirot at a party was a great sight. His faultless evening clothes, the exquisite set of his white tie, the exact symmetry of his hair parting, the sheen of pomade on his hair, and the tortured splendor of his famous mustaches—all combined to paint the perfect picture of an inveterate dandy. It was hard, at these moments, to take the little man seriously.

It was about half-past eleven when Lady Chatterton, bearing down upon us, whisked Poirot neatly out of an admiring group, and carried him off—I need hardly say, with myself in tow.

"I want you to go into my little room upstairs," said Lady Chatterton rather breathlessly as soon as she was out of earshot of her other guests. "You know where it is, M. Poirot. You'll find someone there who needs your help very badly—and you will help her, I know. She's one of my dearest friends—so don't say no."

Energetically leading the way as she talked, Lady Chatterton flung open a door, exclaiming

as she did so, "I've got him, Marguerita darling.
And he'll do anything you want. You *will* help
Mrs. Clayton, won't you, M. Poirot?"

And taking the answer for granted, she withdrew with the same energy that characterized all
her movements.

Mrs. Clayton had been sitting in a chair by
the window. She rose now and came toward us.
Dressed in deep mourning, the dull black showed
up her fair coloring. She was a singularly lovely
woman, and there was about her a simple childlike
candor which made her charm quite irresistible.

"Alice Chatterton is so kind," she said. "She
arranged this. She said you would help me, M.
Poirot. Of course I don't know whether you will
or not—but I hope you will."

She had held out her hand and Poirot had taken
it. He held it now for a moment or two while he
stood scrutinizing her closely. There was nothing
ill-bred in his manner of doing it. It was more the
kind but searching look that a famous consultant
gives a new patient as the latter is ushered into his
presence.

"Are you sure, madame," he said at last, "that
I can help you?"

"Alice says so."

"Yes, but I am asking you, madame."

A little flush rose to her cheeks.

"I don't know what you mean."

"What is it, madame, that you want me to do?"

"You—you—know who I am?" she asked.

"Assuredly."

"Then you can guess what it is I am asking
you to do, M. Poirot—Captain Hastings"—I was

gratified that she realized my identity—"Major Rich did *not* kill my husband."

"Why not?"

"I beg your pardon?"

Poirot smiled at her slight discomfiture.

"I said, 'Why not?' " he repeated.

"I'm not sure that I understand."

"Yet it is very simple. The police—the lawyers—they will all ask the same question: Why did Major Rich kill M. Clayton? I ask the opposite. I ask you, madame, why did Major Rich *not* kill Major Clayton?"

"You mean—why I'm so sure? Well, but I *know*. I know Major Rich so well."

"You know Major Rich so well," repeated Poirot tonelessly.

The color flamed into her cheeks.

"Yes, that's what they'll say—what they'll think! Oh, I know!"

"C'est vrai. That is what they will ask you about—how well you knew Major Rich. Perhaps you will speak the truth, perhaps you will lie. It is very necessary for a woman to lie sometimes. Women must defend themselves—and the lie, it is a good weapon. But there are three people, madame, to whom a woman should speak the truth. To her father confessor, to her hairdresser and to her private detective—if she trusts him. Do you trust me, madame?"

Marguerita Clayton drew a deep breath. "Yes," she said. "I do. I must," she added rather childishly.

"Then, how well do you know Major Rich?"

She looked at him for a moment in silence, then she raised her chin defiantly.

"I will answer your question. I loved Jack from the first moment I saw him—two years ago. Lately I think—I believe—he has come to love me. But he has never said so."

"*Épatant!*" said Poirot. "You have saved me a good quarter of an hour by coming to the point without beating the bush. You have the good sense. Now your husband—did he suspect your feelings?"

"I don't know," said Marguerita slowly. "I thought—lately—that he might. His manner has been different. . . . But that may have been merely my fancy."

"Nobody else knew?"

"I do not think so."

"And—pardon me, madame—you did not love your husband?"

There were, I think, very few women who would have answered that question as simply as this woman did. They would have tried to explain their feelings.

Marguerita Clayton said quite simply: "No."

"*Bien.* Now we know where we are. According to you, madame, Major Rich did not kill your husband, but you realize that all the evidence points to his having done so. Are you aware, privately, of any flaw in that evidence?"

"No. I know nothing."

"When did your husband first inform you of his visit to Scotland?"

"Just after lunch. He said it was a bore, but

he'd have to go. Something to do with land values, he said it was."

"And after that?"

"He went out—to his club, I think. I—I didn't see him again."

"Now as to Major Rich—what was his manner that evening? Just as usual?"

"Yes, I think so."

"You are not sure?"

Marguerita wrinkled her brows.

"He was—a little constrained. With me—not with the others. But I thought I knew why that was. You understand? I am sure the constraint or—or—absentmindedness perhaps describes it better—had nothing to do with Edward. He was surprised to hear that Edward had gone to Scotland, but not unduly so."

"And nothing else unusual occurs to you in connection with that evening?"

Marguerita thought.

"No, nothing whatever."

"You—noticed the chest?"

She shook her head with a little shiver.

"I don't even remember it—or what it was like. We played poker most of the evening."

"Who won?"

"Major Rich. I had very bad luck, and so did Major Curtiss. The Spences won a little, but Major Rich was the chief winner."

"The party broke up—when?"

"About half-past twelve, I think. We all left together."

"Ah!"

Poirot remained silent, lost in thought.

"I wish I could be more helpful to you," said Mrs. Clayton. "I seem to be able to tell you so little."

"About the present—yes. What about the past, madame?"

"The past?"

"Yes. Have there not been incidents?"

She flushed.

"You mean that dreadful little man who shot himself. It wasn't my fault, M. Poirot. Indeed it wasn't."

"It was not precisely of that incident that I was thinking."

"That ridiculous duel? But Italians do fight duels. I was so thankful the man wasn't killed."

"It must have been a relief to you," agreed Poirot gravely.

She was looking at him doubtfully. He rose and took her hand in his.

"I shall not fight a duel for you, madame," he said. "But I will do what you have asked me. I will discover the truth. And let us hope that your instincts are correct—that the truth will help and not harm you."

Our first interview was with Major Curtiss. He was a man of about forty, of soldierly build, with very dark hair and a bronzed face. He had known the Claytons for some years and Major Rich also. He confirmed the press reports.

Clayton and he had had a drink together at the club just before half-past seven, and Clayton had then announced his intention of looking in on

Major Rich on his way to Euston.

"What was Mr. Clayton's manner? Was he depressed or cheerful?"

The major considered. He was a slow-spoken man.

"Seemed in fairly good spirits," he said at last.

"He said nothing about being on bad terms with Major Rich?"

"Good Lord, no. They were pals."

"He didn't object to—his wife's friendship with Major Rich?"

The major became very red in the face.

"You've been reading those damned newspapers, with their hints and lies. Of course he didn't object. Why, he said to me: 'Marguerita's going, of course.' "

"I see. Now during the evening—the manner of Major Rich—was that much as usual?"

"I didn't notice any difference."

"And madame? She, too, was as usual."

"Well," he reflected, "now I come to think of it, she was a bit quiet. You know, thoughtful and faraway."

"Who arrived first?"

"The Spences. They were there when I got there. As a matter of fact, I'd called round for Mrs. Clayton, but found she'd already started. So I got there a bit late."

"And how did you amuse yourselves? You danced? You played the cards?"

"A bit of both. Danced first of all."

"There were five of you?"

"Yes, but that's all right, because I don't dance. I put on the records and the others danced."

"Who danced most with whom?"

"Well, as a matter of fact the Spences like dancing together. They've got a sort of craze on it—fancy steps and all that."

"So that Mrs. Clayton danced mostly with Major Rich?"

"That's about it."

"And then you played poker?"

"Yes."

"And when did you leave?"

"Oh, quite early. A little after midnight."

"Did you all leave together?"

"Yes. As a matter of fact, we shared a taxi, dropped Mrs. Clayton first, then me, and the Spences took it on to Kensington."

Our next visit was to Mr. and Mrs. Spence. Only Mrs. Spence was at home, but her account of the evening tallied with that of Major Curtiss except that she displayed a slight acidity concerning Major Rich's luck at cards.

Earlier in the morning Poirot had had a telephone conversation with Inspector Japp, of Scotland Yard. As a result we arrived at Major Rich's rooms and found his manservant, Burgoyne, expecting us.

The valet's evidence was very precise and clear.

Mr. Clayton had arrived at twenty minutes to eight. Unluckily Major Rich had just that very minute gone out. Mr. Clayton had said that he couldn't wait, as he had to catch a train, but he would just scrawl a note. He accordingly went into the sitting room to do so. Burgoyne had not actually heard his master come in, as he was running the bath, and Major Rich, of course, let himself in

with his own key. In his opinion it was about ten
minutes later that Major Rich called him and sent
him out for cigarettes. No, he had not gone into
the sitting room. Major Rich had stood in the
doorway. He had returned with the cigarettes five
minutes later and on this occasion he had gone
into the sitting room, which was then empty, save
for his master, who was standing by the window
smoking. His master had inquired if his bath were
ready and on being told it was had proceeded to
take it. He, Burgoyne, had not mentioned Mr.
Clayton, as he assumed that his master had found
Mr. Clayton there and let him out himself. His
master's manner had been precisely the same as
usual. He had taken his bath, changed, and
shortly after, Mr. and Mrs. Spence had arrived,
to be followed by Major Curtiss and Mrs.
Clayton.

It had not occurred to him, Burgoyne explained, that Mr. Clayton might have left before
his master's return. To do so, Mr. Clayton would
have had to bang the front door behind him and
that the valet was sure he would have heard.

Still in the same impersonal manner, Burgoyne
proceeded to his finding of the body. For the first
time my attention was directed to the fatal chest.
It was a good-sized piece of furniture standing
against the wall next to the phonograph cabinet.
It was made of some dark wood and plentifully
studded with brass nails. The lid opened simply
enough. I looked in and shivered. Though well
scrubbed, ominous stains remained.

Suddenly Poirot uttered an exclamation.
"Those holes there—they are curious. One would

say that they had been newly made."

The holes in question were at the back of the chest against the wall. There were three or four of them. They were about a quarter of an inch in diameter and certainly had the effect of having been freshly made.

Poirot bent down to examine them, looking inquiringly at the valet.

"It's certainly curious, sir. I don't remember ever seeing those holes in the past, though maybe I wouldn't notice them."

"It makes no matter," said Poirot.

Closing the lid of the chest, he stepped back into the room until he was standing with his back against the window. Then he suddenly asked a question.

"Tell me," he said. "When you brought the cigarettes into your master that night, was there not something out of place in the room?"

Burgoyne hesitated for a minute, then with some slight reluctance he replied,

"It's odd your saying that, sir. Now you come to mention it, there was. That screen there that cuts off the draft from the bedroom door—it was moved a bit more to the left."

"Like this?"

Poirot darted nimbly forward and pulled at the screen. It was a handsome affair of painted leather. It already slightly obscured the view of the chest, and as Poirot adjusted it, it hid the chest altogether.

"That's right, sir," said the valet. "It was like that."

"And the next morning?"

"It was still like that. I remember. I moved it away and it was then I saw the stain. The carpet's gone to be cleaned, sir. That's why the boards are bare."

Poirot nodded.

"I see," he said. "I thank you."

He placed a crisp piece of paper in the valet's palm.

"Thank you, sir."

"Poirot," I said when we were out in the street, "that point about the screen—is that a point helpful to Rich?"

"It is a further point against him," said Poirot ruefully. "The screen hid the chest from the room. It also hid the stain on the carpet. Sooner or later the blood was bound to soak through the wood and stain the carpet. The screen would prevent discovery for the moment. Yes—but there is something there that I do not understand. The valet, Hastings, the valet."

"What about the valet? He seemed a most intelligent fellow."

"As you say, most intelligent. Is it credible, then, that Major Rich failed to realize that the valet would certainly discover the body in the morning? Immediately after the deed he had no time for anything—granted. He shoves the body into the chest, pulls the screen in front of it and goes through the evening hoping for the best. But after the guests are gone? Surely, then is the time to dispose of the body."

"Perhaps he hoped the valet wouldn't notice the stain?"

"That, *mon ami*, is absurd. A stained carpet is

the first thing a good servant would be bound to notice. And Major Rich, he goes to bed and snores there comfortably and does nothing at all about the matter. Very remarkable and interesting, that."

"Curtiss might have seen the stains when he was changing the records the night before?" I suggested.

"That is unlikely. The screen would throw a deep shadow just there. No, but I begin to see. Yes, dimly I begin to see."

"See what?" I asked eagerly.

"The possibilities, shall we say, of an alternative explanation. Our next visit may throw light on things."

Our next visit was to the doctor who had examined the body. His evidence was a mere recapitulation of what he had already given at the inquest. Deceased had been stabbed to the heart with a long thin knife something like a stiletto. The knife had been left in the wound. Death had been instantaneous. The knife was the property of Major Rich and usually lay on his writing table. There were no fingerprints on it, the doctor understood. It had been either wiped or held in a handkerchief. As regards time, any time between seven and nine seemed indicated.

"He could not, for instance, have been killed after midnight?" asked Poirot.

"No. That I can say. Ten o'clock at the outside —but seven-thirty to eight seems clearly indicated."

"There *is* a second hypothesis possible," Poirot said when we were back home. "I wonder if you see it, Hastings. To me it is very plain, and I only need one point to clear up the matter for good and all.''

"It's no good,'' I said. "I'm not there.''

"But make an effort, Hastings. Make an effort.''

"Very well,'' I said. "At seven-forty Clayton is alive and well. The last person to see him alive is Rich—''

"So we assume.''

"Well, isn't it so?''

"You forget, *mon ami*, that Major Rich denies that. He states explicitly that Clayton had gone when he came in.''

"But the valet says that he would have heard Clayton leave because of the bang of the door. And also, if Clayton had left, when did he return? He couldn't have returned after midnight because the doctor says positively that he was dead at least two hours before that. That only leaves one alternative.''

"Yes, *mon ami?*'' said Poirot.

"That in the five minutes Clayton was alone in the sitting room, someone else came in and killed him. But there we have the same objection. Only someone with a key could come in without the valet's knowing, and in the same way the murderer on leaving would have had to bang the door, and that again the valet would have heard.''

"Exactly,'' said Poirot. "And therefore—''

"And therefore—nothing,'' I said. "I can see no other solution.''

"It is a pity,'' murmured Poirot. "And it is

really so exceedingly simple—as the clear blue eyes
of Madame Clayton.''

"You really believe—''

"I believe nothing—until I have got proof. One
little proof will convince me.''

He took up the telephone and called Japp at
Scotland Yard.

Twenty minutes later we were standing before a
little heap of assorted objects laid out on a table.
They were the contents of the dead man's pockets.

There was a handkerchief, a handful of loose
change, a pocketbook containing three pounds ten
shillings, a couple of bills and a worn snapshot of
Marguerita Clayton. There was also a pocket-
knife, a gold pencil and a cumbersome wooden
tool.

It was on this latter that Poirot swooped. He
unscrewed it and several small blades fell out.

"You see, Hastings, a gimlet and all the rest of
it. Ah! it would be a matter of a very few minutes
to bore a few holes in the chest with this.''

"Those holes we saw?''

"Precisely.''

"You mean it was Clayton who bored them
himself?''

"*Mais, oui—mais, oui!* What did they suggest
to you, those holes? They were not to *see* through,
because they were at the back of the chest. What
were they for, then? Clearly for air? But you do
not make air holes for a dead body, so clearly they
were *not* made by the murderer. They suggest one
thing—and one thing only—that a man was going
to *hide* in that chest. And at once, on that hypoth-

esis, things become intelligible. Mr. Clayton is
jealous of his wife and Rich. He plays the old, old
trick of pretending to go away. He watches Rich
go out, then he gains admission, is left alone to
write a note, quickly bores those holes and hides
inside the chest. His wife is coming there that
night. Possibly Rich will put the others off, possibly she will remain after the others have gone, or
pretend to go and return. Whatever it is, Clayton
will *know*. Anything is preferable to the ghastly
torment of suspicion he is enduring.''

"Then you mean that Rich killed him *after* the
others had gone? But the doctor said that was impossible.''

"Exactly. So you see, Hastings, he must have
been killed *during* the evening.''

"But everyone was in the room!''

"Precisely," said Poirot gravely. "You see the
beauty of that? 'Everyone was in the room.' What
an alibi! What sangfroid—what nerve—what au-
dacity!''

"I still don't understand.''

"Who went behind that screen to wind up the
phonograph and change the records? The phonograph and the chest were side by side, remember.
The others are dancing—the phonograph is playing. And the man who does not dance lifts the lid
of the chest and thrusts the knife he has just
slipped into his sleeve deep into the body of the
man who was hiding there.''

"Impossible! The man would cry out.''

"Not if he were drugged first?''

"Drugged?''

"Yes. Who did Clayton have a drink with at

seven-thirty? Ah! Now you see. Curtiss! Curtiss
has inflamed Clayton's mind with suspicions
against his wife and Rich. Curtiss suggests this
plan—the visit to Scotland, the concealment in the
chest, the final touch of moving the screen. Not so
that Clayton can raise the lid a little and get
relief—no, so that he, Curtiss, can raise that lid
unobserved. The plan is Curtiss', and observe the
beauty of it, Hastings. If Rich had observed the
screen was out of place and moved it back—well,
no harm is done. He can make another plan.
Clayton hides in the chest, the mild narcotic that
Curtiss had administered takes effect. He sinks
into unconsciousness. Curtiss lifts up the lid and
strikes—and the phonograph goes on playing
Walking My Baby Back Home.''

I found my voice. ''Why? But why?''

Poirot shrugged his shoulders.

''Why did a man shoot himself? Why did two
Italians fight a duel? Curtiss is of a dark passionate temperament. He wanted Marguerita Clayton.
With her husband and Rich out of the way, she
would, or so he thought, turn to him.''

He added musingly:

''These simple childlike women . . . they are
very dangerous. But *mon Dieu!* what an artistic
masterpiece! It goes to my heart to hang a man
like that. I may be a genius myself, but I am
capable of recognizing genius in other people. A
perfect murder, *mon ami.* I, Hercule Poirot, say it
to you. A perfect murder. *Épatant!*''

Hercule Poirot arranged his letters in a neat pile in front of him. He picked up the topmost letter, studied the address for a moment, then neatly slit the back of the envelope with a little paper knife that he kept on the breakfast table for that express purpose and extracted the contents. Inside was yet another envelope, carefully sealed with purple wax and marked "Private and Confidential."

Hercule Poirot's eyebrows rose a little on his egg-shaped head. He murmured, *"Patience! Nous allons arriver!"* and once more brought the little paper knife into play. This time the envelope yielded a letter—written in a rather shaky and spiky handwriting. Several words were heavily underlined.

Hercule Poirot unfolded it and read. The letter was headed once again "Private and Confidential." On the right-hand side was the address

—Rosebank, Charman's Green, Bucks—and the date—March twenty-first.

> *Dear M. Poirot:* I have been recommended
> to you by an old and valued friend of mine
> who knows the *worry* and *distress* I have been
> in lately. Not that this friend knows the actual
> *circumstances*—those I have kept *entirely* to
> myself—the matter being strictly private. My
> friend assures me that you are *discretion*
> itself—and that there will be no fear of my
> being involved in a *police* matter which, if my
> suspicions should prove correct, I should *very
> much dislike*. But it is of course possible that
> I am *entirely* mistaken. I do not feel myself
> clear-headed enough nowadays—suffering
> as I do from insomnia and the result of a
> severe illness last winter—to investigate
> things for myself. I have neither the *means*
> nor the *ability*. On the other hand, I must
> reiterate once more that this is a very delicate
> family matter and that for many reasons I
> may want the *whole thing hushed up*. If I am
> once assured of the *facts*, I can deal with the
> matter myself and should prefer to do so. I
> hope that I have made myself clear on this
> point. If you will undertake this investiga-
> tion, perhaps you will let me know to the
> above address?
>
> Yours very truly,
AMELIA BARROWBY.

Poirot read the letter through twice. Again his

eyebrows rose slightly. Then he placed it on one side and proceeded to the next envelope in the pile.

At ten o'clock precisely he entered the room where Miss Lemon, his confidential secretary, sat awaiting her instructions for the day. Miss Lemon was forty-eight and of unprepossessing appearance. Her general effect was that of a lot of bones flung together at random. She had a passion for order almost equaling that of Poirot himself; and though capable of thinking, she never thought unless told to do so.

Poirot handed her the morning correspondence. "Have the goodness, mademoiselle, to write refusals couched in correct terms to all of these."

Miss Lemon ran an eye over the various letters, scribbling in turn a hieroglyphic on each of them. These marks were legible to her alone and were in a code of her own: "Soft soap"; "slap in the face"; "purr purr"; "curt"; and so on. Having done this, she nodded and looked up for further instructions.

Poirot handed her Amelia Barrowby's letter. She extracted it from its double envelope, read it through and looked up inquiringly.

"Yes, M. Poirot?" Her pencil hovered—ready —over her shorthand pad.

"What is your opinion of that letter, Miss Lemon?"

With a slight frown Miss Lemon put down the pencil and read through the letter again.

The contents of a letter meant nothing to Miss Lemon except from the point of view of composing an adequate reply. Very occasionally her em-

ployer appealed to her human, as opposed to
her official, capacities. It slightly annoyed Miss
Lemon when he did so—she was very nearly the
perfect machine, completely and gloriously unin-
terested in all human affairs. Her real passion in
life was the perfection of a filing system beside
which all other filing systems should sink into
oblivion. She dreamed of such a system at night.
Nevertheless, Miss Lemon was perfectly capable
of intelligence on purely human matters, as Hercule Poirot well knew.

"Well?" he demanded.

"Old lady," said Miss Lemon. "Got the wind
up pretty badly."

"Ah! The wind rises in her, you think?"

Miss Lemon, who considered that Poirot had
been long enough in Great Britain to understand
its slang terms, did not reply. She took a brief look
at the double envelope.

"Very hush-hush," she said. "And tells you
nothing at all."

"Yes," said Hercule Poirot. "I observed that."

Miss Lemon's hand hung once more hopefully
over the shorthand pad. This time Hercule Poirot
responded.

"Tell her I will do myself the honor to call upon
her at any time she suggests, unless she prefers to
consult me here. Do not type the letter—write it by
hand."

"Yes, M. Poirot."

Poirot produced more correspondence. "These
are bills."

Miss Lemon's efficient hands sorted them
quickly. "I'll pay all but these two."

"Why those two? There is no error in them."

"They are firms you've only just begun to deal with. It looks bad to pay too promptly when you've just opened an account—looks as though you were working up to get some credit later on."

"Ah!" murmured Poirot. "I bow to your superior knowledge of the British tradesman."

"There's nothing much I don't know about them," said Miss Lemon grimly.

The letter to Miss Amelia Barrowby was duly written and sent, but no reply was forthcoming. Perhaps, thought Hercule Poirot, the old lady had unraveled her mystery herself. Yet he felt a shade of surprise that in that case she should not have written a courteous word to say that his services were no longer required.

It was five days later when Miss Lemon, after receiving her morning's instructions, said, "That Miss Barrowby we wrote to—no wonder there's been no answer. She's dead."

Hercule Poirot said very softly, "Ah—dead." It sounded not so much like a question as an answer.

Opening her handbag, Miss Lemon produced a newspaper cutting. "I saw it in the tube and tore it out."

Just registering in his mind approval of the fact that, though Miss Lemon used the word "tore," she had neatly cut the entry out with scissors, Poirot read the announcement taken from the Births, Deaths and Marriages in the *Morning Post:* "On March 26th—suddenly—at Rosebank, Charman's Green, Amelia Jane Barrowby, in her seventy-third year. No flowers, by request.''

Poirot read it over. He murmured under his breath, ''Suddenly.'' Then he said briskly, ''If you will be so obliging as to take a letter, Miss Lemon?''

The pencil hovered. Miss Lemon, her mind dwelling on the intricacies of the filing system, took down in rapid and correct shorthand:

> *Dear Miss Barrowby:* I have received no reply from you, but as I shall be in the neighborhood of Charman's Green on Friday, I will call upon you on that day and discuss more fully the matter you mentioned to me in your letter.
>
> Yours, etc.

''Type this letter, please; and if it is posted at once, it should get to Charman's Green tonight.''

On the following morning a letter in a black-edged envelope arrived by the second post:

> *Dear Sir:* In reply to your letter my aunt, Miss Barrowby, passed away on the twenty-sixth, so the matter you speak of is no longer of importance.
>
> Yours truly,
> MARY DELAFONTAINE.

Poirot smiled to himself. ''No longer of importance. . . . Ah—that is what we shall see. *En avant*—to Charman's Green.''

Rosebank was a house that seemed likely to live up to its name, which is more than can be said for most houses of its class and character.

Hercule Poirot paused as he walked up the path to the front door and looked approvingly at the neatly planned beds on either side of him. Rose trees that promised a good harvest later in the year, and at present daffodils, early tulips, blue hyacinths—the last bed was partly edged with shells.

Poirot murmured to himself, "How does it go, the English rhyme the children sing?

> Mistress Mary, quite contrary,
> How does your garden grow?
> With cockle-shells, and silver bells,
> And pretty maids all in a row.

"Not a row, perhaps," he considered, "but here is at least one pretty maid to make the little rhyme come right."

The front door had opened and a neat little maid in cap and apron was looking somewhat dubiously at the spectacle of a heavily mustached foreign gentleman talking aloud to himself in the front garden. She was, as Poirot had noted, a very pretty little maid, with round blue eyes and rosy cheeks.

Poirot raised his hat with courtesy and addressed her: "Pardon, but does a Miss Amelia Barrowby live here?"

The little maid gasped and her eyes grew rounder. "Oh, sir, didn't you know? She's dead. Ever so sudden it was. Tuesday night."

She hesitated, divided between two strong instincts: the first, distrust of a foreigner; the second, the pleasurable enjoyment of her class in dwelling on the subject of illness and death.

"You amaze me," said Hercule Poirot, not very truthfully. "I had an appointment with the lady for today. However, I can perhaps see the other lady who lives here."

The little maid seemed slightly doubtful. "The mistress? Well, you could see her, perhaps, but I don't know whether she'll be seeing anyone or not."

"She will see me," said Poirot, and handed her a card.

The authority of his tone had its effect. The rosy-cheeked maid fell back and ushered Poirot into a sitting room on the right of the hall. Then, card in hand, she departed to summon her mistress.

Hercule Poirot looked round him. The room was a perfectly conventional drawing room—oatmeal-colored paper with a frieze round the top, indeterminate cretonnes, rose-colored cushions and curtains, a good many china knick-knacks and ornaments. There was nothing in the room that stood out, that announced a definite personality.

Suddenly Poirot, who was very sensitive, felt eyes watching him. He wheeled round. A girl was standing in the entrance of the French window—a small, sallow girl, with very black hair and suspicious eyes.

She came in, and as Poirot made a little bow she burst out abruptly, "Why have you come?"

Poirot did not reply. He merely raised his eyebrows.

"You are not a lawyer—no?" Her English was

good, but not for a minute would anyone have taken her to be English.

"Why should I be a lawyer, mademoiselle?"

The girl stared at him sullenly. "I thought you might be. I thought you had come perhaps to say that she did not know what she was doing. I have heard of such things—the not due influence; that is what they call it, no? But that is not right. She wanted me to have the money, and I shall have it. If it is needful I shall have a lawyer of my own. The money is mine. She wrote it down so, and so it shall be." She looked ugly, her chin thrust out, her eyes gleaming.

The door opened and a tall woman entered and said, "Katrina."

The girl shrank, flushed, muttered something and went out through the window.

Poirot turned to face the newcomer who had so effectually dealt with the situation by uttering a single word. There had been authority in her voice, and contempt and a shade of well-bred irony. He realized at once that this was the owner of the house, Mary Delafontaine.

"M. Poirot? I wrote to you. You cannot have received my letter."

"Alas, I have been away from London."

"Oh, I see; that explains it. I must introduce myself. My name is Delafontaine. This is my husband. Miss Barrowby was my aunt."

Mr. Delafontaine had entered so quietly that his arrival had passed unnoticed. He was a tall man with grizzled hair and an indeterminate manner. He had a nervous way of fingering his chin. He looked often toward his wife, and it was plain that he expected her to take the lead in any conversation.

"I much regret that I intrude in the midst of your bereavement," said Hercule Poirot.

"I quite realize that it is not your fault," said Mrs. Delafontaine. "My aunt died on Tuesday evening. It was quite unexpected."

"Most unexpected," said Mr. Delafontaine. "Great blow." His eyes watched the window where the foreign girl had disappeared.

"I apologize," said Hercule Poirot. "And I withdraw." He moved a step toward the door.

"Half a sec," said Mr. Delafontaine. "You—er—had an appointment with Aunt Amelia, you say?"

"Parfaitement."

"Perhaps you will tell us about it," said his wife. "If there is anything we can do—"

"It was of a private nature," said Poirot. "I am a detective," he added simply.

Mr. Delafontaine knocked over a little china figure he was handling. His wife looked puzzled.

"A detective? And you had an appointment with auntie? But how extraordinary!" She stared at him. "Can't you tell us a little more, M. Poirot? It—it seems quite fantastic."

Poirot was silent for a moment. He chose his words with care.

"It is difficult for me, madame, to know what to do."

"Look here," said Mr. Delafontaine. "She didn't mention Russians, did she?"

"Russians?"

"Yes, you know—Bolshies, Reds, all that sort of thing."

"Don't be absurd, Henry," said his wife.

Mr. Delafontaine collapsed. "Sorry—sorry—I just wondered."

Mary Delafontaine looked frankly at Poirot. Her eyes were very blue—the color of forget-me-nots. "If you can tell us anything, M. Poirot, I should be glad if you would do so. I can assure you that I have a—a reason for asking."

Mr. Delafontaine looked alarmed. "Be careful, old girl—you know there may be nothing in it."

Again his wife quelled him with a glance. "Well, M. Poirot?"

Slowly, gravely, Hercule Poirot shook his head. He shook it with visible regret, but he shook it. "At present, madame," he said, "I fear I must say nothing."

He bowed, picked up his hat and moved to the door. Mary Delafontaine came with him into the hall. On the doorstep he paused and looked at her.

"You are fond of your garden, I think, madame?"

"I? Yes, I spend a lot of time gardening."

"Je vous fait mes compliments."

He bowed once more and strode down to the gate. As he passed out of it and turned to the right he glanced back and registered two impressions —a sallow face watching him from a first-floor window, and a man of erect and soldierly carriage pacing up and down on the opposite side of the street.

Hercule Poirot nodded to himself. *"Definitive-*

ment," he said. "There is a mouse in this hole! What move must the cat make now?"

His decision took him to the nearest post office. Here he put through a couple of telephone calls. The result seemed to be satisfactory. He bent his steps to Charman's Green police station, where he inquired for Inspector Sims.

Inspector Sims was a big, burly man with a hearty manner. "M. Poirot?" he inquired. "I thought so. I've just this minute had a telephone call through from the chief constable about you. He said you'd be dropping in. Come into my office."

The door shut, the inspector waved Poirot to one chair, settled himself in another, and turned a gaze of acute inquiry upon his visitor.

"You're very quick onto the mark, M. Poirot. Come to see us about this Rosebank case almost before we know it is a case. What put you onto it?"

Poirot drew out the letter he had received and handed it to the inspector. The latter read it with some interest.

"Interesting," he said. "The trouble is, it might mean so many things. Pity she couldn't have been a little more explicit. It would have helped us now."

"Or there might have been no need for help."

"You mean?"

"She might have been alive."

"You go as far as that, do you? H'm—I'm not sure you're wrong."

"I pray of you, inspector, recount to me the facts. I know nothing at all."

"That's easily done. Old lady was taken bad after dinner on Tuesday night. Very alarming. Convulsions—spasms—what not. They sent for the doctor. By the time he arrived she was dead. Idea was she'd died of a fit. Well, he didn't much like the look of things. He hemmed and hawed and put it with a bit of soft sawder, but he made it clear that he couldn't give a death certificate. And as far as the family go, that's where the matter stands. They're awaiting the result of the post-mortem. We've got a bit farther. The doctor gave us the tip right away—he and the police surgeon did the autopsy together—and the result is in no doubt whatever. The old lady died of a large dose of strychnine."

"Aha!"

"That's right. Very nasty bit of work. Point is, who gave it to her? It must have been administered very shortly before death. First idea was it was given to her in her food at dinner—but, frankly, that seems to be a washout. They had artichoke soup, served from a tureen, fish pie and apple tart."

" 'They' being?"

"Miss Barrowby, Mr. Delafontaine and Mrs. Delafontaine. Miss Barrowby had a kind of nurse-attendant—a half Russian girl—but she didn't eat with the family. She had the remains as they came out from the dining room. There's a maid, but it was her night out. She left the soup on the stove and the fish pie in the oven, and the apple tart was cold. All three of them ate the same thing—and, apart from that, I don't think you could get strychnine down anyone's throat that way. Stuff's as bitter as gall. The doctor told me you could taste it in a solution of one in a thousand, or something like that.''

"Coffee?"

"Coffee's more like it, but the old lady never took coffee.''

"I see your point. Yes, it seems an insuperable difficulty. What did she drink at the meal?''

"Water."

"Worse and worse."

"Bit of a teaser, isn't it?"

"She had money, the old lady?"

"Very well to do, I imagine. Of course, we haven't got exact details yet. The Delafontaines are pretty badly off, from what I can make out. The old lady helped with the upkeep of the house.''

Poirot smiled a little. He said, "So you suspect the Delafontaines. Which of them?''

"I don't exactly say I suspect either of them in particular. But there it is; they're her only near relations, and her death brings them a tidy sum of money, I've no doubt. We all know what human nature is!''

"Sometimes inhuman—yes, that is very true. And there was nothing else the old lady ate or drank?''

"Well, as a matter of fact—"

"Ah, *voilà!* I felt that you had something, as you say, up your sleeve—the soup, the fish pie, the apple tart—a *bêtise!* Now we come to the hub of the affair.''

"I don't know about that. But as a matter of fact, the old girl took a cachet before meals. You know, not a pill or a tablet; one of those rice-paper things with a powder inside. Some perfectly harmless thing for the digestion.''

"Admirable. Nothing is easier than to fill a cachet with strychnine and substitute it for one of the others. It slips down the throat with a drink of water and is not tasted.''

"That's all right. The trouble is, the girl gave it to her.''

"The Russian girl?''

"Yes. Katrina Rieger. She was a kind of lady-help, nurse-companion to Miss Barrowby. Fairly ordered about by her, too, I gather. Fetch this, fetch that, fetch the other, rub my back, pour out my medicine, run round to the chemist—all that sort of business. You know how it is with these old women—they mean to be kind, but what they need is a sort of black slave!''

Poirot smiled.

"And there you are, you see,'' continued Inspector Sims. "It doesn't fit in what you might call nicely. Why should the girl poison her? Miss Barrowby dies and now the girl will be out of a job, and jobs aren't so easy to find—she's not trained or anything.''

"Still,'' suggested Poirot, "if the box of cachets was left about, anyone in the house might have the opportunity.''

"Naturally we're onto that, M. Poirot. I don't mind telling you we're making our inquiries—quiet like, if you understand me. When the prescription was last made up, where it was usually kept; patience and a lot of spade work—that's what will do the trick in the end. And then there's

Miss Barrowby's solicitor. I'm having an interview with him tomorrow. And the bank manager. There's a lot to be done still.''

Poirot rose. "A little favor, Inspector Sims; you will send me a little word how the affair marches. I would esteem it a great favor. Here is my telephone number.''

"Why, certainly, M. Poirot. Two heads are better than one; and besides, you ought to be in on this, having had that letter and all.''

"You are too amiable, inspector." Politely, Poirot shook hands and took his leave.

He was called to the telephone on the following afternoon. "Is that M. Poirot? Inspector Sims here. Things are beginning to sit up and look pretty in that little matter you and I know of.''

"In verity? Tell me, I pray of you.''

"Well, here's item No. 1—and a pretty big item. Miss B. left a small legacy to her niece and everything else to K. In consideration of her great kindness and attention—that's the way it was put. That alters the complexion of things.''

A picture rose swiftly in Poirot's mind. A sullen face and a passionate voice saying, "The money is mine. She wrote it down and so it shall be." The legacy would not come as a surprise to Katrina—she knew about it beforehand.

"Item No. 2," continued the voice of Inspector Sims. "Nobody but K. handled that cachet.''

"You can be sure of that?''

"The girl herself doesn't deny it. What do you think of that?''

"Extremely interesting.''

"We only want one thing more—evidence of how the strychnine came into her possession. That oughtn't to be difficult.''

"But so far you haven't been successful?"

"I've barely started. The inquest was only this morning."

"What happened at it?"

"Adjourned for a week."

"And the young lady—K.?"

"I'm detaining her on suspicion. Don't want to run any risks. She might have some funny friends in the country who'd try to get her out of it."

"No," said Poirot. "I do not think she has any friends."

"Really? What makes you say that, M. Poirot?"

"It is just an idea of mine. There were no other 'items,' as you call them?"

"Nothing that's strictly relevant. Miss B. seems to have been monkeying about a bit with her shares lately—must have dropped quite a tidy sum. It's rather a funny business, one way and another, but I don't see how it affects the main issue—not at present, that is."

"No, perhaps you are right. Well, my best thanks to you. It was most amiable of you to ring me up."

"Not at all. I'm a man of my word. I could see you were interested. Who knows, you may be able to give me a helping hand before the end."

"That would give me great pleasure. It might help you, for instance, if I could lay my hand on a friend of the girl Katrina."

"I thought you said she hadn't got any

friends?'' said Inspector Sims, surprised.

"I was wrong," said Hercule Poirot. "She has one."

Before the inspector could ask a further question, Poirot had rung off.

With a serious face he wandered into the room where Miss Lemon sat at her typewriter. She raised her hands from the keys at her employer's approach and looked at him inquiringly.

"I want you," said Poirot, "to figure to yourself a little history."

Miss Lemon dropped her hands into her lap in a resigned manner. She enjoyed typing, paying bills, filing papers and entering up engagements. To be asked to imagine herself in hypothetical situations bored her very much, but she accepted it as a disagreeable part of a duty.

"You are a Russian girl," began Poirot.

"Yes," said Miss Lemon, looking intensely British.

"You are alone and friendless in this country. You have reasons for not wishing to return to Russia. You are employed as a kind of drudge, nurse-attendant and companion to an old lady. You are meek and uncomplaining."

"Yes," said Miss Lemon obediently, but entirely failing to see herself being meek to any old lady under the sun.

"The old lady takes a fancy to you. She decides to leave her money to you. She tells you so." Poirot paused.

Miss Lemon said "Yes" again.

"And then the old lady finds out something; perhaps it is a matter of money—she may find that you have not been honest with her. Or it might be more grave still—a medicine that tasted different, some food that disagreed. Anyway, she begins to suspect you of something and she writes to a very famous detective—*enfin*, to the most famous detective—me! I am to call upon her shortly. And then, as you say, the dripping will be in the fire. The great thing is to act quickly. And so—before the great detective arrives—the old lady is dead. And the money comes to you. . . . Tell me, does that seem to you reasonable?"

"Quite reasonable," said Miss Lemon. "Quite reasonable for a Russian, that is. Personally, I should never take a post as a companion. I like my duties clearly defined. And of course I should not dream of murdering anyone."

Poirot sighed. "How I miss my friend Hastings. He had such an imagination. Such a romantic mind! It is true that he always imagined wrong—but that in itself was a guide."

Miss Lemon was silent. She had heard about Captain Hastings before, and was not interested. She looked longingly at the typewritten sheet in front of her.

"So it seems to you reasonable," mused Poirot.

"Doesn't it to you?"

"I am almost afraid it does," sighed Poirot.

The telephone rang and Miss Lemon went out of the room to answer it. She came back to say, "It's Inspector Sims again."

Poirot hurried to the instrument. " 'Allo, 'allo. What is that you say?"

Sims repeated his statement. "We've found a packet of strychnine in the girl's bedroom—

tucked underneath the mattress. The sergeant's just come in with the news. That about clinches it, I think.''

"Yes," said Poirot, "I think that clinches it.'' His voice had changed. It rang with sudden confidence.

When he had rung off, he sat down at his writing table and arranged the objects on it in a mechanical manner. He murmured to himself, "There was something wrong. I felt it—no, not felt. It must have been something I saw. *En avant*, the little gray cells. Ponder—reflect. Was everything logical and in order? The girl—her anxiety about the money; Mme. Delafontaine; her husband—his suggestion of Russians—imbecile, but he is an imbecile; the room; the garden—ah! Yes, the garden.''

He sat up very stiff. The green light shone in his eyes. He sprang up and went into the adjoining room.

"Miss Lemon, will you have the kindness to leave what you are doing and make an investigation for me?''

"An investigation, M. Poirot? I'm afraid I'm not very good—''

Poirot interrupted her. "You said one day that you know all about tradesmen.''

"Certainly I do," said Miss Lemon with confidence.

"Then the matter is simple. You are to go to Charman's Green and you are to discover a fishmonger.''

"A fishmonger?'' asked Miss Lemon, surprised.

"Precisely. The fishmonger who supplied Rose-bank with fish. When you have found him you will ask him a certain question."

He handed her a slip of paper. Miss Lemon took it, noted its contents without interest, then nodded and slipped the lid on her typewriter.

"We will go to Charman's Green together," said Poirot. "You to the fishmonger and I to the police station. It will take us but half an hour from Baker Street."

On arrival at his destination, he was greeted by the surprised Inspector Sims. "Well, this is quick work, M. Poirot. I was talking to you on the phone only an hour ago."

"I have a request to make to you; that you allow me to see this girl Katrina—what is her name?"

"Katrina Rieger. Well, I don't suppose there's any objection to that."

The girl Katrina looked even more sallow and sullen than ever.

Poirot spoke to her very gently. "Mademoi-selle, I want you to believe that I am not your enemy. I want you to tell me the truth."

Her eyes snapped defiantly. "I have told the truth. To everyone I have told the truth! If the old lady was poisoned, it was not I who poisoned her. It is all a mistake. You wish to prevent me having the money." Her voice was rasping. She looked, he thought, like a miserable little cornered rat.

"Tell me about this cachet, mademoiselle," M. Poirot went on. "Did no one handle it but you?"

"I have said so, have I not? They were made up at the chemist's that afternoon. I brought them back with me in my bag—that was just before supper. I opened the box and gave Miss Barrowby one with a glass of water.''

''No one touched them but you?''

''No.'' A cornered rat—with courage!

''And Miss Barrowby had for supper only what we have been told. The soup, the fish pie, the tart?''

''Yes.'' A hopeless ''yes''—dark, smoldering eyes that saw no light anywhere.

Poirot patted her shoulder. ''Be of good courage, mademoiselle. There may yet be freedom—yes, and money—a life of ease.''

She looked at him suspiciously.

As he went out Sims said to him, ''I didn't quite get what you said through the telephone—something about the girl having a friend.''

''She has one. Me!'' said Hercule Poirot, and had left the police station before the inspector could pull his wits together.

At the Green Cat tearooms, Miss Lemon did not keep her employer waiting. She went straight to the point.

''The man's name is Rudge, in the High Street, and you were quite right. A dozen and a half exactly. I've made a note of what he said.'' She handed it to him.

''Arrr.'' It was a deep, rich sound like the purr of a cat.

Hercule Poirot betook himself to Rosebank. As he stood in the front garden, the sun setting behind him, Mary Delafontaine came out to him.

"M. Poirot?" Her voice sounded surprised. "You have come back?"

"Yes, I have come back." He paused and then said, "When I first came here, madame, the children's nursery rhyme came into my head:

> Mistress Mary, quite contrary,
> How does your garden grow?
> With cockle-shells, and silver bells,
> And pretty maids all in a row.

Only they are not *cockle* shells, are they, madame? They are *oyster* shells." His hand pointed.

He heard her catch her breath and then stay very still. Her eyes asked a question.

He nodded. "*Mais, oui*, I know! The maid left the dinner ready—she will swear and Katrina will swear that that is all you had. Only you and your husband know that you brought back a dozen and a half oysters—a little treat *pour la bonne tante*. So easy to put the strychnine in an oyster. It is swallowed—*comme ça!* But there remain the shells—they must not go in the bucket. The maid would see them. And so you thought of making an edging of them to a bed. But there were not enough—the edging is not complete. The effect is bad—it spoils the symmetry of the otherwise charming garden. Those few oyster shells struck an alien note—they displeased my eye on my first visit."

Mary Delafontaine said, "I suppose you guessed from the letter. I knew she had written —but I didn't know how much she'd said."

Poirot answered evasively, "I knew at least that

it was a family matter. If it had been a question of
Katrina there would have been no point in hushing
things up. I understand that you or your husband
handled Miss Barrowby's securities to your own
profit, and that she found out—"

Mary Delafontaine nodded. "We've done it for
years—a little here and there. I never realized she
was sharp enough to find out. And then I learned
she had sent for a detective; and I found out, too,
that she was leaving her money to Katrina—that
miserable little creature!"

"And so the strychnine was put in Katrina's
bedroom? I comprehend. You save yourself and
your husband from what I may discover, and you
saddle an innocent child with murder. Had you no
pity, madame?"

Mary Delafontaine shrugged her shoulders—
her blue forget-me-not eyes looked into Poirot's.
He remembered the perfection of her acting the
first day he had come and the bungling attempts
of her husband. A woman above the average—but
inhuman.

She said, "Pity? For that miserable intriguing
little rat?" Her contempt rang out.

Hercule Poirot said slowly, "I think, madame,
that you have cared in your life for two things
only. One is your husband."

He saw her lips tremble.

"And the other—is your garden."

He looked round him. His glance seemed to
apologize to the flowers for that which he had
done and was about to do.

Problem
at Pollensa Bay

The steamer from Barcelona to Majorca landed Mr. Parker Pyne at Palma in the early hours of the morning—and straightaway he met with disillusionment. The hotels were full! The best that could be done for him was an airless cupboard overlooking an inner court in a hotel in the center of the town—and with that Mr. Parker Pyne was not prepared to put up. The proprietor of the hotel was indifferent to his disappointment.

"What will you?" he observed with a shrug.

Palma was popular now! The exchange was favorable! Everyone—the English, the Americans—they all came to Majorca in the winter. The whole place was crowded. It was doubtful if the English gentleman would be able to get in anywhere—except perhaps at Formentor where the prices were so ruinous that even foreigners blenched at them.

Mr. Parker Pyne partook of some coffee and a roll and went out to view the cathedral, but found himself in no mood for appreciating the beauties of architecture.

He next had a conference with a friendly taxi driver in inadequate French interlarded with native Spanish, and they discussed the merits and possibilities of Soller, Aleudia, Pollensa and Formentor—where there were fine hotels but very expensive.

Mr. Parker Pyne was goaded to inquire how expensive.

They asked, said the taxi driver, an amount that it would be absurd and ridiculous to pay—was it not well known that the English came here because prices were cheap and reasonable?

Mr. Parker Pyne said that that was quite so, but all the same what sums *did* they charge at Formentor?

A price incredible!

Perfectly—but WHAT PRICE EXACTLY?

The driver consented at last to reply in terms of figures.

Fresh from the exactions of hotels in Jerusalem and Egypt, the figure did not stagger Mr. Parker Pyne unduly.

A bargain was struck, Mr. Parker Pyne's suitcases were loaded on the taxi in a somewhat haphazard manner, and they started off to drive round the island, trying cheaper hostelries en route but with the final objective of Formentor.

But they never reached that final abode of plutocracy, for after they had passed through the narrow streets of Pollensa and were following the curved line of the seashore, they came to the Hotel Pino d'Oro—a small hotel standing on the edge of the sea looking out over a view that in the misty haze of a fine morning had the exquisite vagueness of a Japanese print. At once Mr. Parker Pyne knew that this, and this only, was what he was looking for. He stopped the taxi, passed through the painted gate with the hope that he would find a resting place.

The elderly couple to whom the hotel belonged knew no English or French. Nevertheless the matter was concluded satisfactorily. Mr. Parker Pyne was allotted a room overlooking the sea, the suitcases were unloaded, the driver congratulated his passenger upon avoiding the monstrous exigencies of "these new hotels," received his fare and departed with a cheerful Spanish salutation.

Mr. Parker Pyne glanced at his watch and perceiving that it was, even now, but a quarter to ten, he went out onto the small terrace now bathed in a dazzling morning light and ordered, for the second time that morning, coffee and rolls.

There were four tables there, his own, one from which breakfast was being cleared away and two occupied ones. At the one nearest him sat a family of father and mother and two elderly daughters—Germans. Beyond them, at the corner of the terrace, sat what were clearly an English mother and son.

The woman was about fifty-five. She had gray hair of a pretty tone—was sensibly but not fashionably dressed in a tweed coat and skirt—and had that comfortable self-possession which marks an Englishwoman used to much traveling abroad.

The young man who sat opposite her might have been twenty-five and he too was typical of his class and age. He was neither good-looking nor plain, tall nor short. He was clearly on the best of terms with his mother—they made little jokes together—and he was assiduous in passing her things.

As they talked, her eye met that of Mr. Parker Pyne. It passed over him with well-bred nonchalance, but he knew that he had been assimilated and labeled.

He had been recognized as English and doubtless, in due course, some pleasant noncommittal remark would be addressed to him.

Mr. Parker Pyne had no particular objection. His own countrymen and women abroad were inclined to bore him slightly, but he was quite willing to pass the time of day in an amiable manner. In a small hotel it caused constraint if one did not do so. This particular woman, he felt sure, had excellent "hotel manners," as he put it.

The English boy rose from his seat, made some laughing remark and passed into the hotel. The woman took her letters and bag and settled herself in a chair facing the sea. She unfolded a copy of the *Continental Daily Mail*. Her back was to Mr. Parker Pyne.

As he drank the last drop of his coffee, Mr. Parker Pyne glanced in her direction, and instantly he stiffened. He was alarmed—alarmed for the peaceful continuance of his holiday! That back was horribly expressive. In his time he had classified many such backs. Its rigidity—the tenseness of its poise—without seeing her face he knew well enough that the eyes were bright with unshed tears—that the woman was keeping herself in hand by a rigid effort.

Moving warily, like a much-hunted animal, Mr. Parker Pyne retreated into the hotel. Not half an hour before he had been invited to sign his name in the book lying on the desk. There it was—a neat signature—C. Parker Pyne, London.

A few lines above Mr. Parker Pyne noticed the entries: Mrs. R. Chester, Mr. Basil Chester— Holm Park, Devon.

Seizing a pen, Mr. Parker Pyne wrote rapidly over his signature. It now read (with difficulty) Christopher Pyne.

If Mrs. R. Chester was unhappy in Pollensa Bay, it was not going to be made easy for her to consult Mr. Parker Pyne.

Already it had been a source of abiding wonder to that gentleman that so many people he had come across abroad should know his name and have noted his advertisements. In England many thousands of people read the *Times* every day and could have answered quite truthfully that they had never heard such a name in their lives. Abroad, he reflected, they read their newspapers more thoroughly. No item, not even the advertisement columns, escaped them.

Already his holidays had been interrupted on several occasions. He had dealt with a whole series of problems from murder to attempted blackmail. He was determined in Majorca to have peace. He felt instinctively that a distressed mother might trouble that peace considerably.

Mr. Parker Pyne settled down at the Pino d'Oro very happily. There was a larger hotel not far off, the Mariposa, where a good many English people stayed. There was also quite an artist colony living all round. You could walk along by the sea to the fishing village where there was a cocktail bar where people met—there were a few shops. It was all very peaceful and pleasant. Girls strolled about in trousers with brightly colored handkerchiefs tied round the upper halves of their bodies. Young men in berets with rather long hair held forth in "Mac's Bar" on such subjects as plastic values and abstraction in art.

On the day after Mr. Parker Pyne's arrival, Mrs. Chester made a few conventional remarks to him on the subject of the view and the likelihood of the weather keeping fine. She then chatted a little with the German lady about knitting, and had a few pleasant words about the sadness of the political situation with two Danish gentlemen who spent their time rising at dawn and walking for eleven hours.

Mr. Parker Pyne found Basil Chester a most likeable young man. He called Mr. Parker Pyne "sir" and listened most politely to anything the older man said. Sometimes the three English people had coffee together after dinner in the evening. After the third day, Basil left the party after ten minutes or so and Mr. Parker Pyne was left tête-à-tête with Mrs. Chester.

They talked about flowers and the growing of them, of the lamentable state of the English pound and of how expensive France had become, and of the difficulty of getting good afternoon tea.

Every evening when her son departed, Mr. Parker Pyne saw the quickly concealed tremor of her lips, but immediately she recovered and discoursed pleasantly on the above-mentioned subjects.

Little by little she began to talk of Basil—of how well he had done at school—"he was in the First XI, you know"—of how everyone liked him, of how proud his father would have been of the boy had he lived, of how thankful she had been that Basil had never been "wild." "Of course I always urge him to be with young people, but he really seems to prefer being with me."

She said it with a kind of nice modest pleasure in the fact.

But for once Mr. Parker Pyne did not make the usual tactful response he could usually achieve so easily. He said instead:

"Oh! well, there seem to be plenty of young people here—not in the hotel, but roundabout."

At that, he noticed, Mrs. Chester stiffened. She said: Of course there were a lot of *Artists*. Perhaps she was very old-fashioned—*real* art, of course, was different, but a lot of young people just made that sort of thing an excuse for lounging about and doing nothing—and the girls drank a lot too much.

On the following day Basil said to Mr. Parker Pyne:

"I'm awfully glad you turned up here, sir—especially for my mother's sake. She likes having you to talk to in the evenings."

"What did you do when you were first here?"

"As a matter of fact we used to play piquet."

"I see."

"Of course one gets rather tired of piquet. As a matter of fact I've got some friends here— frightfully cheery crowd. I don't really think my mother approves of them—" He laughed as though he felt this ought to be amusing. "The mater's very old-fashioned. . . . Even girls in trousers shock her!"

"Quite so," said Mr. Parker Pyne.

"What I tell her is—one's got to move with the times. . . . The girls at home round us are frightfully dull. . . ."

"I see," said Mr. Parker Pyne.

All this interested him well enough. He was a spectator of a miniature drama, but he was not called upon to take part in it.

And then the worst—from Mr. Parker Pyne's point of view—happened. A gushing lady of his acquaintance came to stay at the Mariposa. They met in the tea shop in the presence of Mrs. Chester.

The newcomer screamed:

"Why—if it isn't Mr. Parker Pyne—the one and only Mr. Parker Pyne! And Adela Chester! Do you know each other? Oh, you do? You're staying at the same hotel? He's the one and only original wizard, Adela—the marvel of the century—all your troubles smoothed out while you wait! What? Didn't you *know?* You must have *heard* about him? Haven't you read his advertisements? *'Are you in trouble? Consult Mr. Parker Pyne.'* There's just nothing he can't do. Husbands and wives flying at each other's throats and he brings 'em together—if you've lost interest in life he gives you the most thrilling adventures. As I say the man's just a *wizard!*"

It went on a good deal longer—Mr. Parker Pyne at intervals making modest disclaimers. He

disliked the look that Mrs. Chester turned upon
him. He disliked even more seeing her return
along the beach in close confabulation with the
garrulous singer of his praises.

The climax came quicker than he expected. That
evening, after coffee, Mrs. Chester said abruptly,

"Will you come into the little salon, Mr. Pyne.
There is something I want to say to you."

He could but bow and submit.

Mrs. Chester's self-control had been wearing
thin—as the door of the little salon closed behind
them, it snapped. She sat down and burst into
tears.

"My boy, Mr. Parker Pyne. You must save
him. *We* must save him. It's breaking my heart!"

"My dear lady, as a mere outsider—"

"Nina Wycherley says you can do *anything*. She
said I was to have the utmost confidence in you.
She advised me to tell you everything—and that
you'd put the whole thing right."

Inwardly Mr. Parker Pyne cursed the obtrusive
Mrs. Wycherley.

Resigning himself he said:

"Well, let us thrash the matter out. A girl, I
suppose?"

"Did he tell you about her?"

"Only indirectly."

Words poured in a vehement stream from Mrs.
Chester. The girl was dreadful. She drank, she
swore—she wore no clothes to speak of. Her sister
lived out here—was married to an artist—a Dutch-
man. The whole set was most undesirable. Half of
them were living together without being married.
Basil was completely changed. He had always

been so quiet, so interested in serious subjects. He had thought at one time of taking up archaeology—"

"Well, well," said Mr. Parker Pyne. "Nature will have her revenge."

"What do you mean?"

"It isn't healthy for a young man to be interested in serious subjects. He ought to be making an idiot of himself over one girl after another."

"Please be serious, Mr. Pyne."

"I'm perfectly serious. Is the young lady, by any chance, the one who had tea with you yesterday?"

He had noticed her—her gray flannel trousers —the scarlet handkerchief tied loosely around her breast—the vermilion mouth and the fact that she had chosen a cocktail in preference to tea.

"You saw her? Terrible! Not the kind of girl Basil has ever admired."

"You haven't given him much chance to admire a girl, have you?"

"I?"

"He's been too fond of *your* company! Bad! However, I daresay he'll get over this—if you don't precipitate matters."

"You don't understand. He wants to marry this girl—Betty Gregg—they're *engaged*."

"It's gone as far as that?"

"Yes. Mr. Parker Pyne, you *must* do something. You must get my boy out of this disastrous marriage! His whole life will be ruined."

"Nobody's life can be ruined except by themselves."

"Basil's will be," said Mrs. Chester positively.

"I'm not worrying about Basil."

"You're not worrying about the *girl?*"

"No, I'm worrying about *you*. You've been squandering your birthright."

Mrs. Chester looked at him, slightly taken aback.

"What are the years from twenty to forty? Fettered and bound by personal and emotional relationships. That's bound to be. That's living. But later there's a new stage. You can think, observe life, discover something about other people and the truth about yourself. Life becomes real—significant. You see it as a whole. Not just one scene—the scene you, as an actor, are playing. No man or woman is actually himself (or herself) till after forty-five. That's when individuality has a chance."

Mrs. Chester said:

"I've been wrapped up in Basil. He's been *everything* to me."

"Well, he shouldn't have been. That's what you're paying for now. Love him as much as you like—but you're Adela Chester, remember, a person—not just Basil's mother."

"It will break my heart if Basil's life is ruined," said Basil's mother.

He looked at the delicate lines of her face, the wistful droop of her mouth. She was, somehow, a lovable woman. He did not want her to be hurt. He said:

"I'll see what I can do."

He found Basil Chester only too ready to talk, eager to urge his point of view.

"This business is being just hellish. Mother's

hopeless—prejudiced, narrow-minded. If only she'd let herself, she'd *see* how fine Betty is."

"And Betty?"

He sighed.

"Betty's being damned difficult! If she'd just conform a bit—I mean leave off the lipstick for a day—it might make all the difference. She seems to go out of her way to be—well—modern—when Mother's about."

Mr. Parker Pyne smiled.

"Betty and Mother are two of the dearest people in the world, I should have thought they would have taken to each other like hot cakes."

"You have a lot to learn, young man," said Mr. Parker Pyne.

"I wish you'd come along and see Betty and have a good talk about it all."

Mr. Parker Pyne accepted the invitation readily.

Betty and her sister and her husband lived in a small dilapidated villa a little way back from the sea. Their life was of a refreshing simplicity. Their furniture comprised three chairs, a table and beds. There was a cupboard in the wall that held the bare requirements of cups and plates. Hans was an excitable young man with wild blond hair that stood up all over his head. He spoke very odd English with incredible rapidity, walking up and down as he did so. Stella, his wife, was small and fair. Betty Gregg had red hair and freckles and a mischievous eye. She was, he noticed, not nearly so made up as she had been the previous day at the Pino d'Oro.

She gave him a cocktail and said with a twinkle:

"You're in on the big bust-up?"

Mr. Parker Pyne nodded.

"And whose side are you on, big boy? The young lovers—or the disapproving dame?"

"May I ask you a question?"

"Certainly."

"Have you been very tactful over all this?"

"Not at all," said Miss Gregg frankly. "But the old cat put my back up" (she glanced round to make sure that Basil was out of earshot). "That woman just makes me feel mad. She's kept Basil tied to her apron strings all these years—that sort of thing makes a man look a fool. Basil isn't a fool really. Then she's so terribly *pukka sahib*."

"That's not really such a bad thing. It's merely 'unfashionable' just at present."

Betty Gregg gave a sudden twinkle.

"You mean it's like putting Chippendale chairs in the attic in Victorian days? Later you get them down again and say, 'Aren't they marvelous?' "

"Something of the kind."

Betty Gregg considered.

"Perhaps you're right. I'll be honest. It was Basil who put my back up—being so anxious about what impression I'd make on his mother. It drove me to extremes. Even now I believe he might give me up—if his mother worked on him good and hard."

"He might," said Mr. Parker Pyne. "If she went about it the right way."

"Are you going to tell her the right way? She won't think of it herself, you know. She'll just go on disapproving and that won't do the trick. But if you prompted her—"

She bit her lip—raised frank blue eyes to his.

"I've heard about you, Mr. Parker Pyne. You're supposed to know something about human nature. Do you think Basil and I could make a go of it—or not?"

"I should like an answer to three questions."

"Suitability test? All right, go ahead."

"Do you sleep with your window open or shut?"

"Open. I like lots of air."

"Do you and Basil enjoy the same kind of food?"

"Yes."

"Do you like going to bed early or late?"

"Really, under the rose, early. At half-past ten I yawn—and I secretly feel rather hearty in the mornings—but of course I daren't admit it."

"You ought to suit each other very well," said Mr. Parker Pyne.

"Rather a superficial test."

"Not at all. I have known seven marriages at least, entirely wrecked, because the husband liked sitting up till midnight and the wife fell asleep at half-past nine and vice versa."

"It's a pity," said Betty, "that everybody can't be happy. Basil and I, and his mother giving us her blessing."

Mr. Parker Pyne coughed.

"I think," he said, "that that could possibly be managed."

She looked at him doubtfully.

"Now I wonder," she said, "if you're double crossing me?"

Mr. Parker Pyne's face told nothing.

To Mrs. Chester he was soothing, but vague. An engagement was not marriage. He himself was going to Soller for a week. He suggested that her line of action should be noncommittal. Let her appear to acquiesce.

He spent a very enjoyable week at Soller.

On his return he found that a totally unexpected development had arisen.

As he entered the Pino d'Oro the first thing he saw was Mrs. Chester and Betty Gregg having tea together. Basil was not there. Mrs. Chester looked haggard. Betty, too, was looking off color. She was hardly made up at all, and her eyelids looked as though she had been crying.

They greeted him in a friendly fashion, but neither of them mentioned Basil.

Suddenly he heard the girl beside him draw in her breath sharply as though something had hurt her. Mr. Parker Pyne turned his head.

Basil Chester was coming up the steps from the sea front. With him was a girl so exotically beautiful that it quite took your breath away. She was dark and her figure was marvelous. No one could fail to notice the fact since she wore nothing but a single garment of pale blue crepe. She was heavily made up with ocher powder and an orange scarlet mouth—but the unguents only displayed her remarkable beauty in a more pronounced fashion. As for young Basil, he seemed unable to take his eyes from her face.

"You're very late, Basil," said his mother. "You were to have taken Betty to Mac's."

"My fault," drawled the beautiful unknown. "We just drifted." She turned to Basil. "Angel—

get me something with a kick in it!''

She tossed off her shoe and stretched out her
manicured toenails which were done emerald
green to match her fingernails.

She paid no attention to the two women, but she
leaned a little towards Mr. Parker Pyne.

"Terrible island this," she said. "I was just
dying with boredom before I met Basil. He *is*
rather a pet!''

"Mr. Parker Pyne—Miss Ramona," said Mrs.
Chester.

The girl acknowledged the introduction with a
lazy smile.

"I guess I'll call you Parker almost at once,"
she murmured. "My name's Dolores."

Basil returned with the drinks. Miss Ramona
divided her conversation (what there was of it—it
was mostly glances) between Basil and Mr. Parker
Pyne. Of the two women she took no notice whatever. Betty attempted once or twice to join in the
conversation but the other girl merely stared at her
and yawned.

Suddenly Dolores rose.

"Guess I'll be going along now. I'm at the other
hotel. Anyone coming to see me home?"

Basil sprang up.

"I'll come with you."

Mrs. Chester said: "Basil, my dear—"

"I'll be back presently, Mother."

"Isn't he the mother's boy?" Miss Ramona
asked of the world at large. "Just toots 'round
after her, don't you?"

Basil flushed and looked awkward. Miss
Ramona gave a nod in Mrs. Chester's direction, a

dazzling smile to Mr. Parker Pyne and she and Basil moved off together.

After they had gone there was rather an awkward silence. Mr. Parker Pyne did not like to speak first. Betty Gregg was twisting her fingers and looking out to sea. Mrs. Chester looked flushed and angry.

Betty said: "Well, what do you think of our new acquisition in Pollensa Bay?" Her voice was not quite steady.

Mr. Parker Pyne said cautiously:

"A little—er—exotic."

"Exotic?" Betty gave a short bitter laugh.

Mrs. Chester said: "She's terrible—terrible. Basil must be quite mad."

Betty said sharply: "Basil's all right."

"Her toenails," said Mrs. Chester with a shiver of nausea.

Betty rose suddenly.

"I think, Mrs. Chester, I'll go home and not stay to dinner after all."

"Oh, my dear—Basil will be so disappointed."

"Will he?" asked Betty with a short laugh. "Anyway, I think I will. I've got rather a headache."

She smiled at them both and went off. Mrs. Chester turned to Mr. Parker Pyne.

"I wish we had never come to this place—never!"

Mr. Parker Pyne shook his head sadly.

"You shouldn't have gone away," said Mrs. Chester. "If you'd been here this wouldn't have happened."

Mr. Parker Pyne was stung to respond,

"My dear lady, I can assure you that when it comes to a question of a beautiful young woman, I should have no influence over your son whatever. He—er—seems to be of a very susceptible nature."

"He never used to be," said Mrs. Chester tearfully.

"Well," said Mr. Parker Pyne with an attempt at cheerfulness, "this new attraction seems to have broken the back of his infatuation for Miss Gregg. That must be some satisfaction to you."

"I don't know what you mean," said Mrs. Chester. "Betty is a dear child and devoted to Basil. She is behaving extremely well over this. I think my boy must be mad."

Mr. Parker Pyne received this startling change of face without wincing. He had met inconsistency in women before. He said mildly:

"Not exactly mad—just bewitched."

"The creature's a Dago. She's impossible."

"But extremely good-looking."

Mrs. Chester snorted.

Basil ran up the steps from the sea front.

"Hullo, Mater, here I am. Where's Betty?"

"Betty's gone home with a headache. I don't wonder."

"Sulking, you mean."

"I consider, Basil, that you are being extremely unkind to Betty."

"For God's sake, Mother, don't jaw. If Betty is going to make this fuss every time I speak to another girl a nice sort of life we'll lead together."

"You *are* engaged."

"Oh, we're engaged all right. That doesn't

mean that we're not going to have any friends of our own. Nowadays people have to lead their own lives and try to cut out jealousy."

He paused.

"Look here, if Betty isn't going to dine with us—I think I'll go back to the Mariposa. They did ask me to dine. . . ."

"Oh, Basil—"

The boy gave her an exasperated look, then ran off down the steps.

Mrs. Chester looked eloquently at Mr. Parker Pyne.

"You see," she said.

He saw.

Matters came to a head a couple of days later. Betty and Basil were to have gone for a long walk, taking a picnic lunch with them. Betty arrived at the Pino d'Oro to find that Basil had forgotten the plan and gone over to Formentor for the day with Dolores Ramona's party.

Beyond a tightening of the lips the girl made no sign. Presently, however, she got up and stood in front of Mrs. Chester (the two women were alone on the terrace).

"It's quite all right," she said. "It doesn't matter. But I think—all the same—that we'd better call the whole thing off."

She slipped from her finger the signet ring that Basil had given her—he would buy the real engagement ring later.

"Will you give him back this, Mrs. Chester? And tell him it's all right—not to worry. . . ."

"Betty dear, don't! He *does* love you—really."

"It looks like it, doesn't it?" said the girl with a

short laugh. "No—I've got some pride. Tell him everything's all right and that I—I wish him luck."

When Basil returned at sunset he was greeted by a storm.

He flushed a little at the sight of his ring.

"So that's how she feels, is it? Well, I daresay it's the best thing."

"Basil!"

"Well, frankly, Mother, we don't seem to have been hitting it off lately."

"Whose fault was that?"

"I don't see that it was mine particularly. Jealousy's beastly and I really don't see why *you* should get all worked up about it. You begged me yourself not to marry Betty."

"That was before I knew her. Basil—my dear— you're not thinking of marrying this other creature."

Basil Chester said soberly:

"I'd marry her like a shot if she'd have me—but I'm afraid she won't."

Cold chills went down Mrs. Chester's spine. She sought and found Mr. Parker Pyne, placidly reading a book in a sheltered corner.

"You must *do* something! You *must* do something! My boy's life will be ruined."

Mr. Parker Pyne was getting a little tired of Basil Chester's life being ruined.

"What can I do?"

"Go and see this terrible creature. If necessary buy her off."

"That may come very expensive."

"I don't care."

"It seems a pity. Still there are, possibly, other ways."

She looked a question. He shook his head.

"I'll make no promises—but I'll see what I can do. I have handled that kind before. By the way, not a word to Basil—that would be fatal."

"Of course not."

Mr. Parker Pyne returned from the Mariposa at midnight. Mrs. Chester was sitting up for him.

"Well?" she demanded breathlessly.

His eyes twinkled.

"The Señorita Dolores Ramona will leave Pollensa tomorrow morning and the island tomorrow night."

"Oh, Mr. Parker Pyne! How did you manage it?"

"It won't cost a cent," said Mr. Parker Pyne. Again his eyes twinkled. "I rather fancied I might have a hold over her—and I was right."

"You are wonderful. Nina Wycherley was quite right. You must let me know—er—your fees—"

Mr. Parker Pyne held up a well-manicured hand.

"Not a penny. It has been a pleasure. I hope all will go well. Of course the boy will be very upset at first when he finds she's disappeared and left no address. Just go easy with him for a week or two."

"If only Betty will forgive him—"

"She'll forgive him all right. They're a nice couple. By the way, I'm leaving tomorrow, too."

"Oh, Mr. Parker Pyne, we shall miss you."

"Perhaps it's just as well I should go before that boy of yours gets infatuated with yet a third girl."

Mr. Parker Pyne leaned over the rail of the

steamer and looked at the lights of Palma. Beside him stood Dolores Ramona. He was saying appreciatively:

"A very nice piece of work, Madeleine. I'm glad I wired you to come out. It's odd when you're such a quiet stay-at-home girl really."

Madeleine de Sara, alias Dolores Ramona, alias Maggie Sayers, said primly: "I'm glad you're pleased, Mr. Parker Pyne. It's been a nice little change. I think I'll go below now and get to bed before the boat starts. I'm such a bad sailor."

A few minutes later a hand fell on Mr. Parker Pyne's shoulder. He turned to see Basil Chester.

"Had to come and see you off, Mr. Parker Pyne, and give you Betty's love and her and my best thanks. It was a grand stunt of yours. Betty and Mother are as thick as thieves. Seemed a shame to deceive the old darling—but she *was* being difficult. Anyway it's all right now. I must just be careful to keep up the annoyance stuff a couple of days longer. We're no end grateful to you, Betty and I."

"I wish you every happiness," said Mr. Parker Pyne.

"Thanks."

There was a pause, then Basil said with somewhat overdone carelessness:

"Is Miss—Miss de Sara—anywhere about? I'd like to thank her, too."

Mr. Parker Pyne shot a keen glance at him.

He said:

"I'm afraid Miss de Sara's gone to bed."

"Oh, too bad—well, perhaps I'll see her in London sometime."

"As a matter of fact she is going to America on business for me almost at once."

"Oh!" Basil's tone was blank. "Well," he said. "I'll be getting along. . . ."

Mr. Parker Pyne smiled. On his way to his cabin he tapped on the door of Madeleine's.

"How are you, my dear? All right? Our young friend has been along. The usual slight attack of Madeleinitis. He'll get over it in a day or two, but you *are* rather distracting."

Yellow Iris

Hercule Poirot stretched out his feet towards the electric radiator set in the wall. Its neat arrangement of red-hot bars pleased his orderly mind.

"A coal fire," he mused to himself, "was always shapeless and haphazard! Never did it achieve the symmetry."

The telephone bell rang. Poirot rose, glancing at his watch as he did so. The time was close on half-past eleven. He wondered who was ringing him up at this hour. It might, of course, be a wrong number.

"And it might," he murmured to himself with a whimsical smile, "be a millionaire newspaper proprietor, found dead in the library of his country house, with a spotted orchid clasped in his left hand and a page torn from a cookery book pinned to his breast."

Smiling at the pleasing conceit, he lifted the receiver.

Immediately a voice spoke—a soft husky woman's voice with a kind of desperate urgency about it.

"Is that M. Hercule Poirot? Is that M. Hercule Poirot?"

"Hercule Poirot speaks."

"M. Poirot—can you come at once—at once— I'm in danger—in great danger—I know it. . . ."

Poirot said sharply,

"Who are you? Where are you speaking from?"

The voice came more faintly but with an even greater urgency.

"At once . . . it's life or death. . . . The Jardin des Cygnes . . . at once . . . table with yellow irises. . . ."

There was a pause—a queer kind of gasp—the line went dead.

Hercule Poirot hung up. His face was puzzled. He murmured between his teeth:

"There is something here very curious."

In the doorway of the Jardin des Cygnes, fat Luigi hurried forward.

"Buona sera, M. Poirot. You desire a table— yes?"

"No, no, my good Luigi. I seek here for some friends. I will look round—perhaps they are not here yet. Ah, let me see, that table there in the corner with the yellow irises—a little question by the way, if it is not indiscreet. On all the other tables there are tulips—pink tulips—why on that one table do you have yellow iris?''

Luigi shrugged his expressive shoulders.

''A command, Monsieur! A special order! Without doubt, the favorite flowers of one of the ladies. That table, it is the table of Mr. Barton Russell—an American—immensely rich.''

''Aha, one must study the whims of the ladies, must one not, Luigi?''

''Monsieur has said it,'' said Luigi.

''I see at that table an acquaintance of mine. I must go and speak to him.''

Poirot skirted his way delicately round the dancing floor on which couples were revolving. The table in question was set for six, but it had at the moment only one occupant, a young man who was thoughtfully, and it seemed pessimistically, drinking champagne.

He was not at all the person that Poirot had expected to see. It seemed impossible to associate the idea of danger or melodrama with any party of which Tony Chapell was a member.

Poirot paused delicately by the table.

''Ah, it is, is it not, my friend Anthony Chapell?''

''By all that's wonderful—Poirot the police hound!'' cried the young man. ''Not Anthony, my dear fellow—Tony to friends!''

He drew out a chair.

''Come, sit with me. Let us discourse of crime! Let us go further and drink to crime.'' He poured champagne into an empty glass. ''But what are you doing in this haunt of song and dance and merriment, my dear Poirot? We have no bodies here, positively not a single body to offer you.''

Poirot sipped the champagne.

"You seem very gay, *mon cher?*"

"Gay? I am steeped in misery—wallowing in gloom. Tell me, you hear this tune they are playing. You recognize it?"

Poirot hazarded cautiously:

"Something perhaps to do with your baby having left you?"

"Not a bad guess," said the young man, "but wrong for once. 'There's nothing like love for making you miserable!' That's what it's called."

"Aha?"

"My favorite tune," said Tony Chapell mournfully. "And my favorite restaurant and my favorite band—and my favorite girl's here and she's dancing it with somebody else."

"Hence the melancholy?" said Poirot.

"Exactly. Pauline and I, you see, have had what the vulgar call words. That is to say, she's had ninety-five words to five of mine out of every hundred. My five are: *'But darling—I can explain.'* —Then she starts in on her ninety-five again and we get no further. I think," added Tony sadly, "that I shall poison myself."

"Pauline?" murmured Poirot.

"Pauline Weatherby. Barton Russell's young sister-in-law. Young, lovely, disgustingly rich. Tonight Barton Russell gives a party. You know him? Big Business, clean-shaven American—full of pep and personality. His wife was Pauline's sister."

"And who else is there at this party?"

"You'll meet 'em in a minute when the music stops. There's Lola Valdez—you know, the South

American dancer in the new show at the Metropole, and there's Stephen Carter. D'you know Carter—he's in the diplomatic service. Very hush-hush. Known as silent Stephen. Sort of man who says, *'I am not at liberty to state, etc., etc.'* Hullo, here they come.''

Poirot rose. He was introduced to Barton Russell, to Stephen Carter, to Señora Lola Valdez, a dark and luscious creature, and to Pauline Weatherby, very young, very fair, with eyes like cornflowers.

Barton Russell said:

"What, is this the great M. Hercule Poirot? I am indeed pleased to meet you, sir. Won't you sit down and join us? That is, unless—"

Tony Chapell broke in.

"He's got an appointment with a body, I believe, or is it an absconding financier, or the Rajah of Borrioboolagah's great ruby?"

"Ah, my friend, do you think I am never off duty? Can I not, for once, seek only to amuse myself?"

"Perhaps you've got an appointment with Carter here. The latest from Geneva. International situation now acute. The stolen plans *must* be found or war will be declared tomorrow!"

Pauline Weatherby said cuttingly:

"Must you be so *completely* idiotic, Tony?"

"Sorry, Pauline."

Tony Chapell relapsed into crestfallen silence.

"How severe you are, Mademoiselle."

"I hate people who play the fool all the time!"

"I must be careful, I see. I must converse only of serious matters."

"Oh, no, M. Poirot. I didn't mean you."

She turned a smiling face to him and asked:

"Are you really a kind of Sherlock Holmes and do wonderful deductions?"

"Ah, the deductions—they are not so easy in real life. But shall I try? Now then, I deduce—that yellow irises are your favorite flowers?"

"Quite wrong, M. Poirot. Lilies of the valley or roses."

Poirot sighed.

"A failure. I will try once more. This evening, not very long ago, you telephoned to someone."

Pauline laughed and clapped her hands.

"Quite right."

"It was not long after you arrived here?"

"Right again. I telephoned the minute I got inside the doors."

"Ah—that is not so good. You telephoned *before* you came to this table?"

"Yes."

"Decidedly very bad."

"Oh, no, I think it was very clever of you. How did you know I had telephoned?"

"That, Mademoiselle, is the great detective's secret. And the person to whom you telephoned —does the name begin with a P—or perhaps with an H?"

Pauline laughed.

"Quite wrong. I telephoned to my maid to post some frightfully important letters that I'd never sent off. Her name's Louise."

"I am confused—quite confused."

The music began again.

"What about it, Pauline?" asked Tony.

"I don't think I want to dance again so soon, Tony."

"Isn't that too bad?" said Tony bitterly to the world at large.

Poirot murmured to the South American girl on his other side:

"Señora, I would not dare to ask you to dance with me. I am too much of the antique."

Lola Valdez said:

"Ah, it ees nonsense that you talk there! You are steel young. Your hair, eet is still black!"

Poirot winced slightly.

"Pauline, as your brother-in-law and your guardian," Barton Russell spoke heavily, "I'm just going to force you onto the floor! This one's a waltz and a waltz is about the only dance I really can do."

"Why, of course, Barton, we'll take the floor right away."

"Good girl, Pauline, that's swell of you."

They went off together. Tony tipped back his chair. Then he looked at Stephen Carter.

"Talkative little fellow, aren't you, Carter?" he remarked. "Help to make a party go with your merry chatter, eh, what?"

"Really, Chapell, I don't know what you mean?"

"Oh, you don't—don't you?" Tony mimicked him.

"My dear fellow."

"Drink, man, drink, if you won't talk."

"No, thanks."

"Then I will."

Stephen Carter shrugged his shoulders.

"Excuse me, must just speak to a fellow I know over there. Fellow I was with at Eton."

Stephen Carter got up and walked to a table a few places away.

Tony said gloomily:

"Somebody ought to drown old Etonians at birth."

Hercule Poirot was still being gallant to the dark beauty beside him.

He murmured:

"I wonder, may I ask, what are the favorite flowers of Mademoiselle?"

"Ah, now, why ees eet you want to know?"

Lola was arch.

"Mademoiselle, if I send flowers to a lady, I am particular that they should be flowers she likes."

"That ees very charming of you, M. Poirot. I weel tell you—I adore the big dark red carnations —or the dark red roses."

"Superb—yes, superb! You do not, then, like yellow flowers—yellow irises?"

"Yellow flowers—no—they do not accord with my temperament."

"How wise. . . . Tell me, Mademoiselle, did you ring up a friend tonight, since you arrived here?"

"I? Ring up a friend? No, what a curious question!"

"Ah, but I, I am a very curious man."

"I'm sure you are." She rolled her dark eyes at him. "A vairy *dan*gerous man."

"No, no, not dangerous; say, a man who may be useful—in danger! You understand?"

Lola giggled. She showed white even teeth.

"No, no," she laughed. "You are dangerous."

Hercule Poirot sighed.

"I see that you do not understand. All this is very strange."

Tony came out of a fit of abstraction and said suddenly:

"Lola, what about a spot of swoop and dip? Come along."

"I weel come—yes. Since M. Poirot ees not brave enough!"

Tony put an arm round her and remarked over his shoulder to Poirot as they glided off:

"You can meditate on crime yet to come, old boy!"

Poirot said: "It is profound what you say there. Yes, it is profound. . . ."

He sat meditatively for a minute or two, then he raised a finger. Luigi came promptly, his wide Italian face wreathed in smiles.

"*Mon vieux*," said Poirot. "I need some information."

"Always at your service, Monsieur."

"I desire to know how many of these people at this table here have used the telephone tonight?"

"I can tell you, Monsieur. The young lady, the one in white, she telephoned at once when she got here. Then she went to leave her cloak and while she was doing that the other lady came out of the cloakroom and went into the telephone box."

"So the Señora *did* telephone! Was that *before* she came into the restaurant?"

"Yes, Monsieur."

"Anyone else?"

"No, Monsieur."

"All this, Luigi, gives me furiously to think!"

"Indeed, Monsieur."

"Yes. I think, Luigi, that *tonight of all nights,* I

must have my wits about me! *Something* is going to happen, Luigi, and I am not at all sure what it is.''

"Anything I can do, Monsieur—"

Poirot made a sign. Luigi slipped discreetly away. Stephen Carter was returning to the table.

"We are still deserted, Mr. Carter," said Poirot.

"Oh—er—quite," said the other.

"You know Mr. Barton Russell well?"

"Yes, known him a good while."

"His sister-in-law, little Miss Weatherby, is very charming."

"Yes, pretty girl."

"You know her well, too?"

"Quite."

"Oh, quite, quite," said Poirot.

Carter stared at him.

The music stopped and the others returned.

Barton Russell said to a waiter:

"Another bottle of champagne—quickly."

Then he raised his glass.

"See here, folks. I'm going to ask you to drink a toast. To tell you the truth, there's an idea back of this little party tonight. As you know, I'd ordered a table for six. There were only five of us. That gave us an empty place. Then, by a very strange coincidence, M. Hercule Poirot happened to pass by and I asked him to join our party.

"You don't know yet what an apt coincidence that was. You see that empty seat tonight represents a lady—the lady in whose memory this party is being given. This party, ladies and gentlemen, is being held in memory of my dear wife—Iris—who died exactly four years ago on this very date!"

There was a startled movement round the table. Barton Russell, his face quietly impassive, raised his glass.

"I'll ask you to drink to her memory. *Iris!*"

"Iris?" said Poirot sharply.

He looked at the flowers. Barton Russell caught his glance and gently nodded his head.

There were little murmurs round the table.

"Iris—Iris. . . ."

Everyone looked startled and uncomfortable.

Barton Russell went on, speaking with his slow monotonous American intonation, each word coming out weightily.

"It may seem odd to you all that I should celebrate the anniversary of a death in this way—by a supper party in a fashionable restaurant. But I have a reason—yes, I have a reason. For M. Poirot's benefit, I'll explain."

He turned his head towards Poirot.

"Four years ago tonight, M. Poirot, there was a supper party held in New York. At it were my wife and myself, Mr. Stephen Carter who was attached to the Embassy in Washington, Mr. Anthony Chapell who had been a guest in our house for some weeks, and Señora Valdez who was at that time enchanting New York City with her dancing. Little Pauline here"—he patted her shoulder—"was only sixteen but she came to the supper party as a special treat. You remember, Pauline?"

"I remember—yes." Her voice shook a little.

"M. Poirot, on that night a tragedy happened. There was a roll of drums and the cabaret started. The lights went down—all but a spotlight in the middle of the floor. When the lights went up again, M. Poirot, my wife was seen to have fallen forward on the table. She was dead—stone dead. There was potassium cyanide found in the dregs of her wine-glass, and the remains of the packet was discovered in her handbag.''

"She had committed suicide?" said Poirot.

"That was the accepted verdict. . . . It broke me up, M. Poirot. There was, perhaps, a possible reason for such an action—the police thought so. I accepted their decision.''

He pounded suddenly on the table.

"But I was not satisfied. . . . No, for four years I've been thinking and brooding—and I'm not satisfied: I don't believe Iris killed herself. I believe, M. Poirot, that she was murdered—by one of those people at the table.''

"Look here, sir—''

Tony Chapell half sprung to his feet.

"Be quiet, Tony," said Russell. "I haven't finished. One of them did it—I'm sure of that now. Someone who, under cover of the darkness, slipped the half emptied packet of cyanide into her handbag. I think I know which of them it was. I mean to know the truth—''

Lola's voice rose sharply.

"You are mad—crazee—who would have harmed her? No, you are mad. Me, I will not stay—''

She broke off. There was a roll of drums.

Barton Russell said:

"The cabaret. Afterwards we will go on with this. Stay where you are, all of you. I've got to go and speak to the dance band. Little arrangement I've made with them.''

He got up and left the table.

"Extraordinary business," commented Carter. "Man's mad."

"He ees crazee, yes," said Lola.

The lights were lowered.

"For two pins I'd clear out," said Tony.

"No!" Pauline spoke sharply. Then she murmured, "Oh, dear—oh, dear—"

"What is it, Mademoiselle?" murmured Poirot.

She answered almost in a whisper.

"It's horrible! It's just like it was that night—"

"Sh! Sh!" said several people.

Poirot lowered his voice.

"A little word in your ear." He whispered, then patted her shoulder. "All will be well," he assured her.

"My God, listen," cried Lola.

"What is it, Señora?"

"*It's the same tune*—the same song that they played that night in New York. Barton Russell must have fixed it. I don't like this."

"Courage—courage—"

There was a fresh hush.

A girl walked out into the middle of the floor, a coal black girl with rolling eyeballs and white glistening teeth. She began to sing in a deep hoarse voice—a voice that was curiously moving.

> I've forgotten you
> I never think of you
> The way you walked
> The way you talked
> The things you used to say
> I've forgotten you

I never think of you
I couldn't say
For sure today
Whether your eyes were blue or gray
I've forgotten you
I never think of you.

I'm through
Thinking of you
I tell you I'm through
Thinking of you . . .
You . . . you . . . you. . . .

The sobbing tune, the deep golden negro voice had a powerful effect. It hypnotized—cast a spell. Even the waiters felt it. The whole room stared at her, hypnotized by the thick cloying emotion she distilled.

A waiter passed softly round the table filling up glasses, murmuring "champagne" in an undertone but all attention was on the one glowing spot of light—the black woman whose ancestors came from Africa, singing in her deep voice:

I've forgotten you
I never think of you
Oh, what a lie
I shall think of you, think of you,
                think of you

Till I die. . . .

The applause broke out frenziedly. The lights went up. Barton Russell came back and slipped into his seat.

"She's great, that girl—" cried Tony.

But his words were cut short by a low cry from Lola.

"Look—look. . . ."

And then they all saw. Pauline Weatherby dropped forward onto the table.

Lola cried:

"She's dead—just like Iris—like Iris in New York."

Poirot sprang from his seat, signing to the others to keep back. He bent over the huddled form, very gently lifted a limp hand and felt for a pulse.

His face was white and stern. The others watched him. They were paralyzed, held in a trance.

Slowly, Poirot nodded his head.

"Yes, she is dead—*la pauvre petite*. And I sitting by her! Ah! but this time the murderer shall not escape."

Barton Russell, his face gray, muttered:

"Just like Iris. . . . She saw something—Pauline saw something that night—Only she wasn't sure —she told me she wasn't sure. . . . We must get the police. . . . Oh, God, little Pauline."

Poirot said:

"Where is her glass?" He raised it to his nose. "Yes, I can smell the cyanide. A smell of bitter almonds . . . the same method, the same poison. . . ."

He picked up her handbag.

"Let us look in her handbag."

Barton Russell cried out:

"You don't believe this is suicide, too? Not on your life."

"Wait," Poirot commanded. "No, there is nothing here. The lights went up, you see, too quickly, the murderer had not time. Therefore, the poison is still on him."

"Or her," said Carter.

He was looking at Lola Valdez.

She spat out:

"What do you mean—what do you say? That I killed her—eet is not true—not true—why should I do such a thing!"

"You had rather a fancy for Barton Russell yourself in New York. That's the gossip I heard. Argentine beauties are notoriously jealous."

"That ees a pack of lies. And I do not come from the Argentine. I come from Peru. Ah—I spit upon you. I—" She relapsed into Spanish.

"I demand silence," cried Poirot. "It is for me to speak."

Barton Russell said heavily:

"Everyone must be searched."

Poirot said calmly,

"*Non, non*, it is not necessary."

"What d'you mean, not necessary?"

"I, Hercule Poirot, know. I see with the eyes of the mind. And I will speak! M. Carter, *will you show us the packet in your breast pocket?*"

"There's nothing in my pocket. What the hell—"

"Tony, my good friend, if you will be so obliging."

Carter cried out:

"Damn you—"

Tony flipped the packet neatly out before Carter could defend himself.

"There you are, M. Poirot, just as you said!"

"It's a damned lie," cried Carter.

Poirot picked up the packet, read the label.

"Cyanide of potassium. The case is complete."

Barton Russell's voice came thickly.

"Carter! I always thought so. Iris was in love with you. She wanted to go away with you. You didn't want a scandal for the sake of your precious career so you poisoned her. You'll hang for this, you dirty dog."

"Silence!" Poirot's voice rang out, firm and authoritative. "This is not finished yet. I, Hercule Poirot, have something to say. My friend here, Tony Chapell, he says to me when I arrive, that I have come in search of crime. That, it is partly true. There *was* crime in my mind—but it was to prevent a crime that I came. And I have prevented it. The murderer, he planned well—but Hercule Poirot he was one move ahead. He had to think fast, and to whisper quickly in Mademoiselle's ear when the lights went down. She is very quick and clever, Mademoiselle Pauline, she played her part well. Mademoiselle, will you be so kind as to show us that you are not dead after all?"

Pauline sat up. She gave an unsteady laugh.

"Resurrection of Pauline," she said.

"Pauline—darling."

"Tony!"

"My sweet."

"Angel."

Barton Russell gasped.

"I—I don't understand. . . ."

"I will help you to understand, Mr. Barton Russell. Your plan has miscarried."

"My plan?"

"Yes, your plan. Who was the only man who had an *alibi* during the darkness. The man who left the table—you, Mr. Barton Russell. But you returned to it under cover of the darkness, circling round it, with a champagne bottle, filling up glasses, putting cyanide in Pauline's glass and dropping the half empty packet in Carter's pocket as you bent over him to remove a glass. Oh, yes, it is easy to play the part of a waiter in darkness when the attention of everyone is elsewhere. That was the real reason for your party tonight. The safest place to commit a murder is in the middle of a crowd."

"What the—why the hell should I want to kill Pauline?"

"It might be, perhaps, a question of money. Your wife left you guardian to her sister. You mentioned that fact tonight. Pauline is twenty. At twenty-one or on her marriage you would have to render an account of your stewardship. I suggest that you could not do that. You have speculated with it. I do not know, Mr. Barton Russell, whether you killed your wife in the same way, or whether her suicide suggested the idea of this crime to you, but I do know that tonight you have been guilty of attempted murder. It rests with Miss Pauline whether you are prosecuted for that."

"No," said Pauline. "He can get out of my sight and out of this country. I don't want a scandal."

"You had better go quickly, Mr. Barton Russell, and I advise you to be careful in future."

Barton Russell got up, his face working.

"To hell with you, you interfering little Belgian jackanapes."

He strode out angrily.

Pauline sighed.

"M. Poirot, you've been wonderful. . . ."

"You, Mademoiselle, you have been the marvelous one. To pour away the champagne, to act the dead body so prettily."

"Ugh," she shivered, "you give me the creeps."

He said gently:

"It was you who telephoned me, was it not?"

"Yes."

"Why?"

"I don't know. I was worried and—frightened without knowing quite why I was frightened. Barton told me he was having this party to commemorate Iris' death. I realized he had some scheme on—but he wouldn't tell me what it was. He looked so—so queer and so excited that I felt something terrible might happen—only of course I never dreamed that he meant to—to get rid of *me*."

"And so, Mademoiselle?"

"I'd heard people talking about you. I thought if I could only get you here perhaps it would stop anything happening. I thought that being a—a foreigner—if I rang up and pretended to be in danger and—and made it sound mysterious—"

"You thought the melodrama, it would attract me? That is what puzzled me. The message itself —definitely it was what you call 'bogus'—it did not ring true. But the fear in the voice—that was real. Then I came—and you denied very categorically having sent me a message."

"I had to. Besides, I didn't want you to know it was me."

"Ah, but I was fairly sure of that! Not at first. But I soon realized that the only two people who could know about the yellow irises on the table were you or Mr. Barton Russell."

Pauline nodded.

"I heard him ordering them to be put on the table," she explained. "That, and his ordering a table for six when I knew only five were coming, made me suspect—"

She stopped, biting her lip.

"What did you suspect, Mademoiselle?"

She said slowly:

"I was afraid—of something happening—to Mr. Carter."

Stephen Carter cleared his throat. Unhurriedly but quite decisively he rose from the table.

"Er—h'm—I have to—er—thank you, Mr. Poirot. I owe you a great deal. You'll excuse me, I'm sure, if I leave you. Tonight's happenings have been—rather upsetting."

Looking after his retreating figure, Pauline said violently:

"I hate him. I've always thought it was—because of him that Iris killed herself. Or perhaps —Barton killed her. Oh, it's all so hateful. . . ."

Poirot said gently:

"Forget, Mademoiselle . . . forget. . . . Let the past go. . . . Think only of the present. . . ."

Pauline murmured, "Yes—you're right. . . ."

Poirot turned to Lola Valdez.

"Señora, as the evening advances I become more brave. If you would dance with me now—"

"Oh, yes, indeed. You are—you are ze cat's

whiskers, M. Poirot. I inseest on dancing with you."

"You are too kind, Señora."

Tony and Pauline were left. They leant towards each other across the table.

"Darling Pauline."

"Oh, Tony, I've been such a nasty spiteful spitfiring little cat to you all day. Can you ever forgive me?"

"Angel! This is Our Tune again. Let's dance."

They danced off, smiling at each other and humming softly:

> There's nothing like Love for making
>   you miserable
> There's nothing like Love for making
>   you blue
> Depressed
> Possessed
> Sentimental
> Temperamental
> There's nothing like Love
> For getting you down.
>
> There's nothing like Love for driving
>   you crazy
> There's nothing like Love for making
>   you mad
> Abusive
> Allusive
> Suicidal
> Homicidal
> There's nothing like Love
> There's nothing like Love. . . .

Miss Marple
Tells a Story

I don't think I've ever told you, my dears—you, Raymond, and you, Joan, about a rather curious little business that happened some years ago now. I don't want to seem *vain* in any way—of course I know that in comparison with you young people I'm not clever at all—Raymond writes those very modern books all about rather unpleasant young men and women—and Joan paints those very remarkable pictures of square people with curious bulges on them—very clever of you, my dear, but as Raymond always says (only quite kindly, because he is the kindest of nephews) I am hopelessly Victorian. I admire Mr. Alma-Tadema and Mr. Frederic Leighton and I suppose to you they seem hopelessly *vieux jeu*. Now let me see, what was I saying? Oh, yes—that I didn't want to appear vain—but I couldn't help being just a teeny weeny bit pleased with myself, because, just by applying a little common sense, I believe I really did solve a problem that had baffled cleverer heads than mine. Though really I should have thought the whole thing was *obvious* from the beginning. . . .

Well, I'll tell you my little story, and if you think I'm inclined to be conceited about it, you must remember that I did at least help a fellow creature who was in very grave distress.

The first I knew of this business was one evening about nine o'clock when Gwen—(you remember Gwen? My little maid with red hair) well —Gwen came in and told me that Mr. Petherick and a gentleman had called to see me. Gwen had showed them into the drawing-room—quite rightly. I was sitting in the dining-room because in early spring I think it is so wasteful to have two fires going.

I directed Gwen to bring in the cherry brandy and some glasses and I hurried into the drawing-room. I don't know whether you remember Mr. Petherick? He died two years ago, but he had been a friend of mine for many years as well as attending to all my legal business. A very shrewd man and a really clever solicitor. His son does my business for me now—a very nice lad and very up to date—but somehow I don't feel quite the *confidence* I had in Mr. Petherick.

I explained to Mr. Petherick about the fires and he said at once that he and his friend would come into the dining-room—and then he introduced his friend—a Mr. Rhodes. He was a youngish man— not much over forty—and I saw at once that there was something very wrong. His manner was most *peculiar*. One might have called it *rude* if one hadn't realized that the poor fellow was suffering from *strain*.

When we were settled in the dining-room and Gwen had brought the cherry brandy, Mr. Petherick explained the reason for his visit.

"Miss Marple," he said, "you must forgive an old friend for taking a liberty. What I have come here for is a consultation."

I couldn't understand at all what he meant, and he went on:

"In a case of illness one likes two points of view—that of the specialist and that of the family physician. It is the fashion to regard the former as of more value, but I am not sure that I agree. The specialist has experience only in his own subject—the family doctor has, perhaps, less knowledge—but a wider experience."

I knew just what he meant, because a young niece of mine not long before had hurried her child off to a very well-known specialist in skin diseases without consulting her own doctor whom she considered an old dodderer, and the specialist had ordered some very expensive treatment, and later they found that all the child was suffering from was rather an unusual form of measles.

I just mention this—though I have a horror of *digressing*—to show that I appreciated Mr. Petherick's point—but I still hadn't any idea of what he was driving at.

"If Mr. Rhodes is ill—" I said, and stopped—because the poor man gave the most dreadful laugh.

He said: "I expect to die of a broken neck in a few months' time."

And then it all came out. There had been a case

of murder lately in Barnchester—a town about
twenty miles away. I'm afraid I hadn't paid much
attention to it at the time, because we had been
having a lot of excitement in the village about our
district nurse, and outside occurrences like an
earthquake in India and a murder in Barnchester,
although of course far more important really—
had given way to our own little local excitements.
I'm afraid villages are like that. Still, I *did*
remember having read about a woman having
been stabbed in a hotel, though I hadn't remembered her name. But now it seemed that this
woman had been Mr. Rhodes' wife—and as if that
wasn't bad enough—he was actually under suspicion of having murdered her himself.

All this Mr. Petherick explained to me very
clearly, saying that, although the Coroner's jury
had brought in a verdict of murder by a person or
persons unknown, Mr. Rhodes had reason to believe that he would probably be arrested within a
day or two, and that he had come to Mr. Petherick
and placed himself in his hands. Mr. Petherick
went on to say that they had that afternoon consulted Sir Malcolm Olde, K.C., and that in the
event of the case coming to trial Sir Malcolm had
been briefed to defend Mr. Rhodes.

Sir Malcolm was a young man, Mr. Petherick
said, very up to date in his methods, and he had
indicated a certain line of defense. But with that
line of defense Mr. Petherick was not entirely
satisfied.

"You see, my dear lady," he said, "it is tainted
with what I call the specialist's point of view. Give
Sir Malcolm a case and he sees only one point—

the most likely line of defense. But even the best line of defense may ignore completely what is, to my mind, the vital point. It takes no account of what actually happened.''

Then he went on to say some very kind and flattering things about my acumen and judgment and my knowledge of human nature, and asked permission to tell me the story of the case in the hopes that I might be able to suggest some explanation.

I could see that Mr. Rhodes was highly skeptical of my being of any use and that he was annoyed at being brought here. But Mr. Petherick took no notice and proceeded to give me the facts of what occurred on the night of March 8th.

Mr. and Mrs. Rhodes had been staying at the Crown Hotel in Barnchester. Mrs. Rhodes who (so I gathered from Mr. Petherick's careful language) was perhaps just a shade of a hypochondriac, had retired to bed immediately after dinner. She and her husband occupied adjoining rooms with a connecting door. Mr. Rhodes, who is writing a book on prehistoric flints, settled down to work in the adjoining room. At eleven o'clock he tidied up his papers and prepared to go to bed. Before doing so, he just glanced into his wife's room to make sure that there was nothing she wanted. He discovered the electric light on and his wife lying in bed stabbed through the heart. She had been dead at least an hour—probably longer. The following were the points made. There was another door in Mrs. Rhodes' room leading into the corridor. This door was locked and bolted on the inside. The only window in the room was closed and latched. According to Mr. Rhodes nobody had passed through the room in which he was sitting except a chambermaid bringing hot water bottles. The weapon found in the wound was a stiletto dagger which had been lying on Mrs. Rhodes' dressing-table. She was in the habit of using it as a paper knife. There were no finger-prints on it.

The situation boiled down to this—no one but Mr. Rhodes and the chambermaid had entered the victim's room.

I inquired about the chambermaid.

"That was our first line of inquiry," said Mr. Petherick. "Mary Hill is a local woman. She has been chambermaid at the Crown for ten years. There seems absolutely no reason why she should commit a sudden assault on a guest. She is, in any case, extraordinarily stupid, almost half-witted. Her story has never varied. She brought Mrs. Rhodes her hot water bottle and says the lady was drowsy—just dropping off to sleep. Frankly, I cannot believe, and I am sure no jury would believe, that she committed the crime."

Mr. Petherick went on to mention a few additional details. At the head of the staircase in the Crown Hotel is a kind of miniature lounge where people sometimes sit and have coffee. A passage goes off to the right and the last door in it is the door into the room occupied by Mr. Rhodes. The passage then turns sharply to the right again and the first door round the corner is the door into Mrs. Rhodes' room. As it happened, both these doors could be seen by witnesses. The first door— that into Mr. Rhodes' room, which I will call A, could be seen by four people, two commercial travelers and an elderly married couple who were having coffee. According to them nobody went in or out of door A except Mr. Rhodes and the chambermaid. As to the other door in passage B, there was an electrician at work there and he also swears that nobody entered or left door B except the chambermaid.

It was certainly a very curious and interesting case. On the face of it, it looked as though Mr. Rhodes *must* have murdered his wife. But I could see that Mr. Petherick was quite convinced of his client's innocence and Mr. Petherick was a very shrewd man.

At the inquest Mr. Rhodes had told a hesitating and rambling story about some woman who had written threatening letters to his wife. His story, I gathered, had been unconvincing in the extreme. Appealed to by Mr. Petherick, he explained himself.

"Frankly," he said, "I never believed it. I thought Amy had made most of it up."

Mrs. Rhodes, I gathered, was one of those romantic liars who go through life embroidering everything that happens to them. The amount of adventures that, according to her own account, happened to her in a year was simply incredible. If she slipped on a bit of banana peel it was a case of near escape from death. If a lamp-shade caught fire, she was rescued from a burning building at the hazard of her life. Her husband got into the habit of discounting her statements. Her tale as to some woman whose child she had injured in a motor accident and who had vowed vengeance on her—well—Mr. Rhodes had simply not taken any notice of it. The incident had happened before he married his wife and although she had read him letters couched in crazy language, he had suspected her of composing them herself. She had actually done such a thing once or twice before. She was a woman of hysterical tendencies who craved ceaselessly for excitement.

Now, all that seemed to me very natural—indeed, we have a young woman in the village who does much the same thing. The danger with such people is that when anything at all extraordinary really does happen to them, nobody believes they are speaking the truth. It seemed to me that that was what had happened in this case. The police, I gathered, merely believed that Mr. Rhodes was making up this unconvincing tale in order to avert suspicion from himself.

I asked if there had been any women staying by themselves in the Hotel. It seems there were two —a Mrs. Granby, an Anglo-Indian widow, and a Miss Carruthers, rather a horsey spinster who dropped her g's. Mr. Petherick added that the most minute inquiries had failed to elicit anyone who had seen either of them near the scene of the crime and there was nothing to connect either of them with it in any way. I asked him to describe their personal appearance. He said that Mrs. Granby had reddish hair rather untidily done, was sallow-faced and about fifty years of age. Her clothes were rather picturesque, being made mostly of native silks, etc. Miss Carruthers was about forty, wore pince-nez, had close-cropped hair like a man and wore mannish coats and skirts.

"Dear me," I said, "that makes it very difficult."

Mr. Petherick looked inquiringly at me, but I didn't want to say any more just then, so I asked what Sir Malcolm Olde had said.

Sir Malcolm Olde, it seemed, was going all out for suicide. Mr. Petherick said the medical evidence was dead against this, and there was the absence of fingerprints, but Sir Malcolm was confident of being able to call conflicting medical testimony and to suggest some way of getting over the fingerprint difficulty. I asked Mr. Rhodes what he thought and he said all doctors were fools but he himself couldn't really believe his wife had killed herself. "She wasn't that kind of woman," he said simply—and I believed him. Hysterical people don't usually commit suicide.

I thought a minute and then I asked if the door from Mrs. Rhodes' room led straight into the corridor. Mr. Rhodes said no—there was a little hallway with bathroom and lavatory. It was the door from the bedroom to the hallway that was locked and bolted on the inside.

"In that case," I said, "the whole thing seems to me remarkably simple."

And really, you know, it *did*. . . . The simplest thing in the world. And yet no one seemed to have seen it that way.

Both Mr. Petherick and Mr. Rhodes were staring at me so that I felt quite embarrassed.

"Perhaps," said Mr. Rhodes, "Miss Marple hasn't quite appreciated the difficulties."

"Yes," I said, "I think I have. There are four possibilities. Either Mrs. Rhodes was killed by her husband, or by the chambermaid, or she committed suicide, or she was killed by an outsider whom nobody saw enter or leave."

"And that's impossible," Mr. Rhodes broke in. "Nobody could come in or go out through my room without my seeing them, and even if anyone did manage to come in through my wife's room without the electrician seeing them, how the devil could they get out again leaving the door locked and bolted on the inside?"

Mr. Petherick looked at me and said: "Well, Miss Marple?" in an encouraging manner.

"I should like," I said, "to ask a question. Mr. Rhodes, what did the chambermaid look like?"

He said he wasn't sure—she was tallish, he thought—he didn't remember if she was fair or dark. I turned to Mr. Petherick and asked him the same question.

He said she was of medium height, had fairish hair and blue eyes and rather a high color.

Mr. Rhodes said: "You are a better observer than I am, Petherick."

I ventured to disagree. I then asked Mr. Rhodes if he could describe the maid in my house. Neither he nor Mr. Petherick could do so.

"Don't you see what that means?" I said. "You both came here full of your own affairs and the person who let you in was only a *parlormaid*. The same applies to Mr. Rhodes at the Hotel. He saw only a *chambermaid*. He saw her uniform and her apron. He was engrossed by his work. But Mr. Petherick has interviewed the same woman in a different capacity. He has looked at her as a *person*.

"That's what the woman who did the murder counted upon."

As they still didn't see, I had to explain.

"I think," I said, "that this is how it went. The chambermaid came in by door A, passed through Mr. Rhodes' room into Mrs. Rhodes' room with the hot water bottle and went out through the hallway into passage B. X—as I will call our murderess—came in by door B into the little hallway, concealed herself in—well, in a certain apartment, ahem—and waited until the chambermaid had passed out. Then she entered Mrs. Rhodes' room, took the stiletto from the dressing-table—(she had doubtless explored the room earlier in the day) went up to the bed, stabbed the dozing woman, wiped the handle of the stiletto, locked and bolted the door by which she had entered, and then passed out through the room where Mr. Rhodes was working."

Mr. Rhodes cried out: "But I should have *seen* her. The electrician would have seen her go in."

"No," I said. "That's where you're wrong. You wouldn't see her—*not if she were dressed as a chambermaid*." I let it sink in, then I went on, "You were engrossed in your work—out of the tail of your eye you saw a chambermaid come in, go into your wife's room, come back and go out. It was the same *dress*—but not the same woman. That's what the people having coffee saw—a chambermaid go in and a chambermaid come out. The electrician did the same. I daresay if a chambermaid were very pretty a gentleman might notice her face—human nature being what it is —but if she were just an ordinary middle-aged woman—well—it would be the chambermaid's *dress* you would see—not the woman herself."

Mr. Rhodes cried: "Who was she?"

"Well," I said, "that is going to be a little difficult. It must be either Mrs. Granby or Miss Carruthers. Mrs. Granby sounds as though she might wear a wig normally—so she could wear her own hair as a chambermaid. On the other hand, Miss Carruthers with her close-cropped mannish head might easily put on a wig to play her part. I daresay you will find out easily enough which of them it is. Personally, I incline myself to think it will be Miss Carruthers."

And really, my dears, that is the end of the story. Carruthers was a false name, but she was the woman all right. There was insanity in her family. Mrs. Rhodes, who was a most reckless and dangerous driver, had run over her little girl, and it had driven the poor woman off her head. She concealed her madness very cunningly except for writing distinctly insane letters to her intended victim. She had been following her about for some time, and she laid her plans very cleverly. The false hair and maid's dress she posted in a parcel first thing the next morning. When taxed with the truth she broke down and confessed at once. The poor thing is in Broadmoor now. Completely unbalanced, of course, but a very cleverly planned crime.

Mr. Petherick came to me afterwards and brought me a very nice letter from Mr. Rhodes—really, it made me blush. Then my old friend said to me: "Just one thing—why did you think it was more likely to be Carruthers than Granby? You'd never seen either of them."

"Well," I said. "It was the g's. You said she dropped her g's. Now, that's done a lot by hunting people in books, but I don't know many people who do it in reality—and certainly no one under sixty. You said this woman was forty. Those dropped g's sounded to me like a woman who was playing a part and overdoing it."

I shan't tell you what Mr. Petherick said to that —but he was very complimentary—and I really couldn't help feeling just a teeny weeny bit pleased with myself.

And it's extraordinary how things turn out for the best in this world. Mr. Rhodes has married again—such a nice, sensible girl—and they've got a dear little baby and—what do you think?—they asked me to be godmother. Wasn't it nice of them?

Now I do hope you don't think I've been running on too long. . . .

The Dream

Hercule Poirot gave the house a steady appraising glance. His eyes wandered a moment to its surroundings, the shops, the big factory building on the right, the blocks of cheap mansion flats opposite.

Then once more his eyes returned to Northway House, relic of an earlier age—an age of space and leisure, when green fields had surrounded its well-bred arrogance. Now it was an anachronism, submerged and forgotten in the hectic sea of modern London, and not one man in fifty could have told you where it stood.

Furthermore, very few people could have told you to whom it belonged, though its owner's name would have been recognized as one of the world's richest men. But money can quench publicity as well as flaunt it. Benedict Farley, that eccentric millionaire, chose not to advertise his choice of residence. He himself was rarely seen, seldom making a public appearance. From time to time he appeared at board meetings, his lean figure, beaked nose, and rasping voice easily dominating the assembled directors. Apart from that, he was just a well-known figure of legend. There were his strange meannesses, his incredible generosities, as well as more personal details—his famous patch-work dressing-gown, now reputed to be twenty-eight years old, his invariable diet of cabbage soup and caviare, his hatred of cats. All these things the public knew.

Hercule Poirot knew them also. It was all he did know of the man he was about to visit. The letter which was in his coat pocket told him little more.

After surveying this melancholy landmark of a past age for a minute or two in silence, he walked up the steps to the front door and pressed the bell, glancing as he did so at the neat wrist-watch which had at last replaced an earlier favorite—the large turnip-faced watch of earlier days. Yes, it was exactly nine-thirty. As ever, Hercule Poirot was exact to the minute.

The door opened after just the right interval. A perfect specimen of the genus butler stood outlined against the lighted hall.

"Mr. Benedict Farley?" asked Hercule Poirot.

The impersonal glance surveyed him from head to foot, inoffensively but effectively.

"En gros et en détail," thought Hercule Poirot to himself with appreciation.

"You have an appointment, sir?" asked the suave voice.

"Yes."

"Your name, sir?"

"M. Hercule Poirot."

The butler bowed and drew back. Hercule Poirot entered the house. The butler closed the door behind him.

But there was yet one more formality before the deft hands took hat and stick from the visitor.

"You will excuse me, sir. I was to ask for a letter."

With deliberation Poirot took from his pocket the folded letter and handed it to the butler. The latter gave it a mere glance, then returned it with a bow. Hercule Poirot returned it to his pocket. Its contents were simple.

Northway House, W.8.

M. HERCULE POIROT.
DEAR SIR,

Mr. Benedict Farley would like to have the benefit of your advice. If convenient to yourself he would be glad if you would call upon him at the above address at 9:30 tomorrow (Thursday) evening.

Yours truly,
HUGO CORNWORTHY.
(Secretary).

P.S.—Please bring this letter with you.

Deftly the butler relieved Poirot of hat, stick, and overcoat. He said:

"Will you please come up to Mr. Cornworthy's room?"

He led the way up the broad staircase. Poirot followed him, looking with appreciation at such *objets d'art* as were of an opulent and florid nature! His taste in art was always somewhat bourgeois.

On the first floor the butler knocked on a door.

Hercule Poirot's eyebrows rose very slightly. It was the first jarring note. For the best butlers do not knock at doors—and yet indubitably this was a first-class butler!

It was, so to speak, the first intimation of contact with the eccentricity of a millionaire.

A voice from within called out something. The butler threw open the door. He announced (and again Poirot sensed the deliberate departure from orthodoxy):

"The gentleman you are expecting, sir."

Poirot passed into the room. It was a fair-sized room, very plainly furnished in a workmanlike fashion. Filing cabinets, books of reference, a couple of easy chairs, and a large and imposing desk covered with neatly docketed papers. The corners of the room were dim, for the only light came from a big green-shaded reading-lamp which stood on a small table by the arm of one of the easy chairs. It was placed so as to cast its full light on anyone approaching from the door. Hercule Poirot blinked a little, realizing that the lamp bulb was at least 150 watts. In the armchair sat a thin figure in a patchwork dressing-gown—Benedict Farley. His head was stuck forward in a characteristic attitude, his beaked nose projecting like that of a bird. A crest of white hair like that of a cockatoo rose above his forehead. His eyes glittered behind thick lenses as he peered suspiciously at his visitor.

"Hey," he said at last—and his voice was shrill and harsh, with a rasping note in it. "So you're Hercule Poirot, hey?"

"At your service," said Poirot politely and bowed, one hand on the back of the chair.

"Sit down—sit down," said the old man testily.

Hercule Poirot sat down—in the full glare of the lamp. From behind it the old man seemed to be studying him attentively.

"How do I know you're Hercule Poirot— hey?" he demanded fretfully. "Tell me that —hey?"

Once more Poirot drew the letter from his pocket and handed it to Farley.

"Yes," admitted the millionaire grudgingly. "That's it. That's what I got Cornworthy to write." He folded it up and tossed it back. "So you're the fellow, are you?"

With a little wave of his hand Poirot said:

"I assure you there is no deception!"

Benedict Farley chuckled suddenly.

"That's what the conjuror says before he takes the goldfish out of the hat! Saying that is part of the trick, you know."

Poirot did not reply. Farley said suddenly:

"Think I'm a suspicious old man, hey? So I am. Don't trust anybody! That's my motto. Can't trust anybody when you're rich. No, no, it doesn't do."

"You wished," Poirot hinted gently, "to consult me?"

The old man nodded.

"That's right. Always buy the best. That's my motto. Go to the expert and don't count the cost. You'll notice, M. Poirot, I haven't asked you your fee. I'm not going to! Send me in the bill later—*I* shan't cut up rough over it. Damned fools at the dairy thought they could charge me two and nine for eggs when two and seven's the market price—lot of swindlers! I won't be swindled. But the man at the top's different. He's worth the money. I'm at the top myself—I know."

Hercule Poirot made no reply. He listened attentively, his head poised a little on one side.

Behind his impassive exterior he was conscious of a feeling of disappointment. He could not exactly put his finger on it. So far Benedict Farley had run true to type—that is, he had conformed to the popular idea of himself; and yet—Poirot was disappointed.

"The man," he said disgustedly to himself, "is a mountebank—nothing but a mountebank!"

He had known other millionaires, eccentric men too, but in nearly every case he had been conscious of a certain force, an inner energy that had commanded his respect. If they had worn a patchwork dressing-gown, it would have been because they liked wearing such a dressing-gown. But the dressing-gown of Benedict Farley, or so it seemed to Poirot, was essentially a stage property. And the man himself was essentially stagey. Every word he spoke was uttered, so Poirot felt assured, sheerly for effect.

He repeated again unemotionally, "You wished to consult me, Mr. Farley?"

Abruptly the millionaire's manner changed.

He leaned forward. His voice dropped to a croak.

"Yes. Yes . . . I want to hear what you've got to say—what you think. . . . Go to the top! That's my way! The best doctor—the best detective—it's between the two of them."

"As yet, Monsieur, I do not understand."

"Naturally," snapped Farley. "I haven't begun to tell you."

He leaned forward once more and shot out an abrupt question.

"What do you know, M. Poirot, about dreams?"

The little man's eyebrows rose. Whatever he had expected, it was not this.

"For that, Monsieur Farley, I should recommend Napoleon's *Book of Dreams*—or the latest practicing psychologist from Harley Street."

Benedict Farley said soberly, "I've tried both. . . ."

There was a pause, then the millionaire spoke, at first almost in a whisper, then with a voice growing higher and higher.

"It's the same dream—night after night. And I'm afraid, I tell you—I'm afraid. . . . It's always the same. I'm sitting in my room next door to this. Sitting at my desk, writing. There's a clock there and I glance at it and see the time—exactly twenty-eight minutes past three. Always the same time, you understand.

"*And when I see the time, M. Poirot, I know I've got to do it*. I don't want to do it—I loathe doing it—but I've got to. . . ."

His voice had risen shrilly.

Unperturbed, Poirot said, "And what is it that you have to do?"

"At twenty-eight minutes past three," Benedict Farley said hoarsely, "I open the second drawer down on the right of my desk, take out the revolver that I keep there, load it and walk over to the window. And then—and then—"

"Yes?"

Benedict Farley said in a whisper:

"Then I shoot myself. . . ."

There was silence.

Then Poirot said, "That is your dream?"

"Yes."

"The same every night?"

"Yes."

"What happens after you shoot yourself?"

"I wake up."

Poirot nodded his head slowly and thoughtfully. "As a matter of interest, do you keep a revolver in that particular drawer?"

"Yes."

"Why?"

"I have always done so. It is as well to be prepared."

"Prepared for what?"

Farley said irritably, "A man in my position has to be on his guard. All rich men have enemies."

Poirot did not pursue the subject. He remained silent for a moment or two, then he said:

"Why exactly did you send for me?"

"I will tell you. First of all I consulted a doctor—three doctors to be exact."

"Yes?"

"The first told me it was all a question of diet.

He was an elderly man. The second was a young man of the modern school. He assured me that it all hinged on a certain event that took place in infancy at that particular time of day—three twenty-eight. I am so determined, he says, not to remember that event, that I symbolize it by destroying myself. That is his explanation.''

"And the third doctor?'' asked Poirot.

Benedict Farley's voice rose in shrill anger.

"He's a young man too. He has a preposterous theory! He asserts that I, myself, am tired of life, that my life is so unbearable to me that I deliberately want to end it! But since to acknowledge that fact would be to acknowledge that essentially I am a failure, I refuse in my waking moments to face the truth. But when I am asleep, all inhibitions are removed, and I proceed to do that *which I really wish to do*. I put an end to myself.''

"His view is that you really wish, unknown to yourself, to commit suicide?'' said Poirot.

Benedict Farley cried shrilly:

"And that's impossible—impossible! I'm perfectly happy! I've got everything I want—everything money can buy! It's fantastic—unbelievable even to suggest a thing like that!''

Poirot looked at him with interest. Perhaps something in the shaking hands, the trembling shrillness of the voice, warned him that the denial was *too* vehement, that its very insistence was in itself suspect. He contented himself with saying:

"And where do I come in, Monsieur?''

Benedict Farley calmed down suddenly. He tapped with an emphatic finger on the table beside him.

"There's another possibility. And if it's right, you're the man to know about it! You're famous, you've had hundreds of cases—fantastic, improbable cases! You'd know if anyone does."

"Know what?"

Farley's voice dropped to a whisper.

"Supposing someone wants to kill me. . . . Could they do it this way? Could they make me dream that dream night after night?"

"Hypnotism, you mean?"

"Yes."

Hercule Poirot considered the question.

"It would be possible, I suppose," he said at last. "It is more a question for a doctor."

"You don't know of such a case in your experience?"

"Not precisely on those lines, no."

"You see what I'm driving at? I'm made to dream the same dream, night after night, night after night—and then—one day the suggestion is too much for me—*and I act upon it*. I do what I've dreamed of so often—kill myself!"

Slowly Hercule Poirot shook his head.

"You don't think that is possible?" asked Farley.

"Possible?" Poirot shook his head. "That is not a word I care to meddle with."

"But you think it improbable?"

"Most improbable."

Benedict Farley murmured, "The doctor said so too. . . ." Then his voice rising shrilly again, he cried out, "But why do I have this dream? Why? Why?"

Hercule Poirot shook his head. Benedict Farley

said abruptly, "You're sure you've never come across anything like this in your experience?"

"Never."

"That's what I wanted to know."

Delicately, Poirot cleared his throat.

"You permit," he said, "a question?"

"What is it? What is it? Say what you like."

"Who is it you suspect of wanting to kill you?"

Farley snapped out, "Nobody. Nobody at all."

"But the idea presented itself to your mind?" Poirot persisted.

"I wanted to know—if it was a possibility."

"Speaking from my own experience, I should say No. Have you ever been hypnotized, by the way?"

"Of course not. D'you think I'd lend myself to such tomfoolery?"

"Then I think one can say that your theory is definitely improbable."

"But the dream, you fool, the dream."

"The dream is certainly remarkable," said Poirot thoughtfully. He paused and then went on. "I should like to see the scene of this drama—the table, the clock, and the revolver."

"Of course, I'll take you next door."

Wrapping the folds of his dressing-gown round him, the old man half-rose from his chair. Then suddenly, as though a thought had struck him, he resumed his seat.

"No," he said. "There's nothing to see there. I've told you all there is to tell."

"But I should like to see for myself—"

"There's no need," Farley snapped. "You've given me your opinion. That's the end."

Poirot shrugged his shoulders. "As you please." He rose to his feet. "I am sorry, Mr. Farley, that I have not been able to be of assistance to you."

Benedict Farley was staring straight ahead of him.

"Don't want a lot of hanky-pankying around," he growled out. "I've told you the facts—you can't make anything of them. That closes the matter. You can send me in a bill for a consultation fee."

"I shall not fail to do so," said the detective dryly. He walked towards the door.

"Stop a minute." The millionaire called him back. "That letter—I want it."

"The letter from your secretary?"

"Yes."

Poirot's eyebrows rose. He put his hand into his pocket, drew out a folded sheet, and handed it to the old man. The latter scrutinized it, then put it down on the table beside him with a nod.

Once more Hercule Poirot walked to the door. He was puzzled. His busy mind was going over and over the story he had been told. Yet in the midst of his mental preoccupation, a nagging sense of something wrong obtruded itself. And that something had to do with himself—not with Benedict Farley.

With his hand on the door knob, his mind cleared. He, Hercule Poirot, had been guilty of an error! He turned back into the room once more.

"A thousand pardons! In the interest of your problem I have committed a folly! That letter I handed to you—by mischance I put my hand into my right-hand pocket instead of the left—"

"What's all this? What's all this?"

"The letter that I handed you just now—an apology from my laundress concerning the treatment of my collars." Poirot was smiling, apologetic. He dipped into his left-hand pocket. "This is *your* letter."

Benedict Farley snatched at it—grunted: "Why the devil can't you mind what you're doing?"

Poirot retrieved his laundress's communication, apologized gracefully once more, and left the room.

He paused for a moment outside on the landing. It was a spacious one. Directly facing him was a big old oak settle with a refectory table in front of it. On the table were magazines. There were also two armchairs and a table with flowers. It reminded him a little of a dentist's waiting-room.

The butler was in the hall below waiting to let him out.

"Can I get you a taxi, sir?"

"No, I thank you. The night is fine. I will walk."

Hercule Poirot paused a moment on the pavement waiting for a lull in the traffic before crossing the busy street.

A frown creased his forehead.

"No," he said to himself. "I do not understand at all. Nothing makes sense. Regrettable to have to admit it, but I, Hercule Poirot, am completely baffled."

That was what might be termed the first act of the drama. The second act followed a week later. It opened with a telephone call from one John Stillingfleet, M.D.

He said with a remarkable lack of medical decorum:

"That you, Poirot, old horse? Stillingfleet here."

"Yes, my friend. What is it?"

"I'm speaking from Northway House—Benedict Farley's."

"Ah, yes?" Poirot's voice quickened with interest. "What of—Mr. Farley?"

"Farley's dead. Shot himself this afternoon."

There was a pause, then Poirot said:

"Yes. . . ."

"I notice you're not overcome with surprise. Know something about it, old horse?"

"Why should you think that?"

"Well, it isn't brilliant deduction or telepathy or anything like that. We found a note from Farley to you making an appointment about a week ago."

"I see."

"We've got a tame police inspector here—got to be careful, you know, when one of these millionaire blokes bumps himself off. Wondered whether you could throw any light on the case. If so, perhaps you'd come round?"

"I will come immediately."

"Good for you, old boy. Some dirty work at the cross-roads—eh?"

Poirot merely repeated that he would set forth immediately.

"Don't want to spill the beans over the telephone? Quite right. So long."

A quarter of an hour later Poirot was sitting in the library, a low long room at the back of Northway House on the ground floor. There were five other persons in the room. Inspector Barnett, Dr. Stillingfleet, Mrs. Farley, the widow of the millionaire, Joanna Farley, his only daughter, and Hugo Cornworthy, his private secretary.

Of these, Inspector Barnett was a discreet soldierly-looking man. Dr. Stillingfleet, whose professional manner was entirely different from his telephonic style, was a tall, long-faced young man of thirty. Mrs. Farley was obviously very much younger than her husband. She was a handsome dark-haired woman. Her mouth was hard and her black eyes gave absolutely no clue to her emotions. She appeared perfectly self-possessed. Joanna Farley had fair hair and a freckled face. The prominence of her nose and chin was clearly inherited from her father. Her eyes were intelligent and shrewd. Hugo Cornworthy was a somewhat colorless young man, very correctly dressed. He seemed intelligent and efficient.

After greetings and introductions, Poirot narrated simply and clearly the circumstances of his visit and the story told him by Benedict Farley. He could not complain of any lack of interest.

"Most extraordinary story I've ever heard!" said the inspector. "A dream, eh? Did you know anything about this, Mrs. Farley?"

She bowed her head.

"My husband mentioned it to me. It upset him very much. I—I told him it was indigestion—his diet, you know, was very peculiar—and suggested his calling in Dr. Stillingfleet."

That young man shook his head.

"He didn't consult me. From M. Poirot's story,

I gather he went to Harley Street.''

"I would like your advice on that point, doctor," said Poirot. "Mr. Farley told me that he consulted three specialists. What do you think of the theories they advanced?"

Stillingfleet frowned.

"It's difficult to say. You've got to take into account that what he passed on to you wasn't exactly what had been said to him. It was a layman's interpretation."

"You mean he had got the phraseology wrong?"

"Not exactly. I mean they would put a thing to him in professional terms, he'd get the meaning a little distorted, and then recast it in his own language."

"So that what he told me was not really what the doctors said."

"That's what it amounts to. He's just got it all a little wrong, if you know what I mean."

Poirot nodded thoughtfully. "Is it known whom he consulted?" he asked.

Mrs. Farley shook her head, and Joanna Farley remarked:

"None of us had any idea he had consulted anyone."

"Did he speak to *you* about his dream?" asked Poirot.

The girl shook her head.

"And you, Mr. Cornworthy?"

"No, he said nothing at all. I took down a letter to you at his dictation, but I had no idea why he wished to consult you. I thought it might possibly have something to do with some business irregularity."

Poirot asked: "And now as to the actual facts of Mr. Farley's death?"

Inspector Barnett looked interrogatively at Mrs. Farley and at Dr. Stillingfleet, and then took upon himself the role of spokesman.

"Mr. Farley was in the habit of working in his own room on the first floor every afternoon. I understand that there was a big amalgamation of businesses in prospect—"

He looked at Hugo Cornworthy who said, "Consolidated Coachlines."

"In connection with that," continued Inspector Barnett, "Mr. Farley had agreed to give an interview to two members of the Press. He very seldom did anything of the kind—only about once in five years, I understand. Accordingly two reporters, one from the Associated Newsgroups, and one from Amalgamated Press-sheets, arrived at a quarter past three by appointment. They waited on the first floor outside Mr. Farley's door—which was the customary place for people to wait who had an appointment with Mr. Farley. At twenty past three a messenger arrived from the office of Consolidated Coachlines with some urgent papers. He was shown into Mr. Farley's room where he handed over the documents. Mr. Farley accompanied him to the door of the room, and from there spoke to the two members of the Press. He said:

" 'I am sorry, gentlemen, to have to keep you waiting, but I have some urgent business to attend to. I will be as quick as I can.'

"The two gentlemen, Mr. Adams and Mr. Stoddart, assured Mr. Farley that they would await his convenience. He went back into his room, shut the door—and was never seen alive again!''

"Continue," said Poirot.

"At a little after four o'clock," went on the inspector, "Mr. Cornworthy here came out of his room which is next door to Mr. Farley's, and was surprised to see the two reporters still waiting. He wanted Mr. Farley's signature to some letters and thought he had also better remind him that these two gentlemen were waiting. He accordingly went into Mr. Farley's room. To his surprise he could not at first see Mr. Farley and thought the room was empty. Then he caught sight of a boot sticking out behind the desk (which is placed in front of the window). He went quickly across and discovered Mr. Farley lying there dead, with a revolver beside him.

"Mr. Cornworthy hurried out of the room and directed the butler to ring up Dr. Stillingfleet. By the latter's advice, Mr. Cornworthy also informed the police."

"Was the shot heard?" asked Poirot.

"No. The traffic is very noisy here, the landing window was open. What with lorries and motor horns it would be most unlikely if it had been noticed."

Poirot nodded thoughtfully. "What time is it supposed he died?" he asked.

Stillingfleet said:

"I examined the body as soon as I got here—that is, at thirty-two minutes past four. Mr. Farley had been dead at least an hour."

Poirot's face was very grave.

"So then, it seems possible that his death could have occurred at the time he mentioned to me—

that is, at twenty-eight minutes past three.''

"Exactly," said Stillingfleet.

"Any finger-marks on the revolver?"

"Yes, his own."

"And the revolver itself?"

The inspector took up the tale.

"Was one which he kept in the second right-hand drawer of his desk, just as he told you. Mrs. Farley has identified it positively. Moreover, you understand, there is only one entrance to the room, the door giving on to the landing. The two reporters were sitting exactly opposite that door and they swear that no one entered the room from the time Mr. Farley spoke to them, until Mr. Cornworthy entered it at a little after four o'clock.''

"So that there is every reason to suppose that Mr. Farley committed suicide?"

Inspector Barnett smiled a little.

"There would have been no doubt at all but for one point."

"And that?"

"The letter written to you."

Poirot smiled too.

"I see! Where Hercule Poirot is concerned—immediately the suspicion of murder arises!"

"Precisely," said the inspector dryly. "However, after your clearing up of the situation—"

Poirot interrupted him. "One little minute." He turned to Mrs. Farley. "Had your husband ever been hypnotized?"

"Never."

"Had he studied the question of hypnotism? Was he interested in the subject?"

She shook her head. "I don't think so."

Suddenly her self-control seemed to break down. "That horrible dream! It's uncanny! That he should have dreamed that—night after night—and then—and then—it's as though he were—*hounded* to death!"

Poirot remembered Benedict Farley saying—*"I proceed to do that which I really wish to do. I put an end to myself."*

He said, "Had it ever occurred to you that your husband might be tempted to do away with himself?"

"No—at least—sometimes he was very queer...."

Joanna Farley's voice broke in clear and scornful. "Father would never have killed himself. He was far too careful of himself."

Dr. Stillingfleet said, "It isn't the people who threaten to commit suicide who usually do it, you know, Miss Farley. That's why suicides sometimes seem unaccountable."

Poirot rose to his feet. "Is it permitted," he asked, "that I see the room where the tragedy occurred?"

"Certainly. Dr. Stillingfleet—"

The doctor accompanied Poirot upstairs.

Benedict Farley's room was a much larger one than the secretary's next door. It was luxuriously furnished with deep leather-covered armchairs, a thick pile carpet, and a superb outsize writing-desk.

Poirot passed behind the latter to where a dark stain on the carpet showed just before the window. He remembered the millionaire saying, *"At twenty-eight minutes past three I open the second*

*drawer down on the right of my desk, take out the
revolver that I keep there, load it, and walk over
to the window. And then—and then I shoot myself.''*

He nodded slowly. Then he said:

''The window was open like this?''

''Yes. But nobody could have got in that way.''

Poirot put his head out. There was no sill or
parapet and no pipes near. Not even a cat could
have gained access that way. Opposite rose the
blank wall of the factory, a dead wall with no windows in it.

Stillingfleet said, ''Funny room for a rich man
to choose as his own sanctum with that outlook.
It's like looking out on to a prison wall.''

''Yes,'' said Poirot. He drew his head in and
stared at the expanse of solid brick. ''I think,'' he
said, ''that that wall is important.''

Stillingfleet looked at him curiously. ''You
mean—psychologically?''

Poirot had moved to the desk. Idly, or so it
seemed, he picked up a pair of what are usually
called lazytongs. He pressed the handles; the tongs
shot out to their full length. Delicately, Poirot
picked up a burnt match stump with them from
beside a chair some feet away and conveyed it
carefully to the waste-paper basket.

''When you've finished playing with those
things . . .'' said Stillingfleet irritably.

Hercule Poirot murmured, ''An ingenious in-
vention,'' and replaced the tongs neatly on the
writing-table. Then he asked:

''Where were Mrs. Farley and Miss Farley at the
time of the—death?''

''Mrs. Farley was resting in her room on the

floor above this. Miss Farley was painting in her studio at the top of the house."

Hercule Poirot drummed idly with his fingers on the table for a minute or two. Then he said:

"I should like to see Miss Farley. Do you think you could ask her to come here for a minute or two?"

"If you like."

Stillingfleet glanced at him curiously, then left the room. In another minute or two the door opened and Joanna Farley came in.

"You do not mind, mademoiselle, if I ask you a few questions?"

She returned his glance coolly. "Please ask anything you choose."

"Did you know that your father kept a revolver in his desk?"

"No."

"Where were you and your mother—that is to say your stepmother—that is right?"

"Yes, Louise is my father's second wife. She is only eight years older than I am. You were about to say—?"

"Where were you and she on Thursday of last week? That is to say, on Thursday night."

She reflected for a minute or two.

"Thursday? Let me see. Oh, yes, we had gone to the theater. To see *Little Dog Laughed*."

"Your father did not suggest accompanying you?"

"He never went out to theaters."

"What did he usually do in the evenings?"

"He sat in here and read."

"He was not a very sociable man?"

The girl looked at him directly. "My father," she said, "had a singularly unpleasant personality. No one who lived in close association with him could possibly be fond of him."

"That, mademoiselle, is a very candid statement."

"I am saving you time, M. Poirot. I realize quite well what you are getting at. My stepmother married my father for his money. I live here because I have no money to live elsewhere. There is a man I wish to marry—a poor man; my father saw to it that he lost his job. He wanted me, you see, to marry well—an easy matter since I was to be his heiress!"

"Your father's fortune passes to you?"

"Yes. That is, he left Louise, my stepmother, a quarter of a million free of tax, and there are other legacies, but the residue goes to me." She smiled suddenly. "So you see, M. Poirot, I had every reason to desire my father's death!"

"I see, mademoiselle, that you have inherited your father's intelligence."

She said thoughtfully, "Father was clever. . . . One felt that with him—that he had force—driving power—but it had all turned sour—bitter—there was no humanity left. . . ."

Hercule Poirot said softly, "*Grand Dieu*, but what an imbecile I am. . . ."

Joanna Farley turned towards the door. "Is there anything more?"

"Two little questions. These tongs here," he picked up the lazytongs, "were they always on the table?"

"Yes. Father used them for picking up things.

He didn't like stooping.''

"One other question. Was your father's eye-sight good?''

She stared at him.

"Oh, no—he couldn't see at all—I mean he couldn't see without his glasses. His sight had always been bad from a boy.''

"But with his glasses?''

"Oh, he could see all right then, of course.''

"He could read newspapers and fine print?''

"Oh, yes.''

"That is all, mademoiselle.''

She went out of the room.

Poirot murmured, "I was stupid. It was there, all the time, under my nose. And because it was so near I could not see it.''

He leaned out of the window once more. Down below, in the narrow way between the house and the factory, he saw a small dark object.

Hercule Poirot nodded, satisfied, and went downstairs again.

The others were still in the library. Poirot addressed himself to the secretary:

"I want you, Mr. Cornworthy, to recount to me in detail the exact circumstances of Mr. Farley's summons to me. When, for instance, did Mr. Farley dictate that letter?''

"On Wednesday afternoon—at five-thirty, as far as I can remember.''

"Were there any special directions about posting it?''

"He told me to post it myself.''

"And you did so?''

"Yes.''

"Did he give any special instructions to the butler about admitting me?"

"Yes. He told me to tell Holmes (Holmes is the butler) that a gentleman would be calling at 9:30. He was to ask the gentleman's name. He was also to ask to see the letter."

"Rather peculiar precautions to take, don't you think?"

Cornworthy shrugged his shoulders.

"Mr. Farley," he said carefully, "was rather a peculiar man."

"Any other instructions?"

"Yes. He told me to take the evening off."

"Did you do so?"

"Yes, immediately after dinner I went to the cinema."

"When did you return?"

"I let myself in about a quarter past eleven."

"Did you see Mr. Farley again that evening?"

"No."

"And he did not mention the matter the next morning?"

"No."

Poirot paused a moment, then resumed, "When I arrived I was not shown into Mr. Farley's own room."

"No. He told me that I was to tell Holmes to show you into my room."

"Why was that? Do you know?"

Cornworthy shook his head. "I never questioned any of Mr. Farley's orders," he said dryly. "He would have resented it if I had."

"Did he usually receive visitors in his own room?"

"Usually, but not always. Sometimes he saw them in my room."

"Was there any reason for that?"

Hugo Cornworthy considered.

"No—I hardly think so—I've never really thought about it."

Turning to Mrs. Farley, Poirot asked:

"You permit that I ring for your butler?"

"Certainly, M. Poirot."

Very correct, very urbane, Holmes answered the bell.

"You rang, madam?"

Mrs. Farley indicated Poirot with a gesture. Holmes turned politely. "Yes, sir?"

"What were your instructions, Holmes, on the Thursday night when I came here?"

Holmes cleared his throat, then said:

"After dinner Mr. Cornworthy told me that Mr. Farley expected a Mr. Hercule Poirot at 9:30. I was to ascertain the gentleman's name, and I was to verify the information by glancing at a letter. Then I was to show him up to Mr. Cornworthy's room."

"Were you also told to knock on the door?"

An expression of distaste crossed the butler's countenance.

"That was one of Mr. Farley's orders. I was always to knock when introducing visitors—business visitors, that is," he added.

"Ah, that puzzled me! Were you given any other instructions concerning me?"

"No, sir. When Mr. Cornworthy had told me what I have just repeated to you he went out."

"What time was that?"

"Ten minutes to nine, sir."

"Did you see Mr. Farley after that?"

"Yes, sir, I took him up a glass of hot water as usual at nine o'clock."

"Was he then in his own room or in Mr. Cornworthy's?"

"He was in his own room, sir."

"You noticed nothing unusual about that room?"

"Unusual? No, sir."

"Where were Mrs. Farley and Miss Farley?"

"They had gone to the theater, sir."

"Thank you, Holmes, that will do."

Holmes bowed and left the room. Poirot turned to the millionaire's widow.

"One more question, Mrs. Farley. Had your husband good sight?"

"No. Not without his glasses."

"He was very short-sighted?"

"Oh, yes, he was quite helpless without his spectacles."

"He had several pairs of glasses?"

"Yes."

"Ah," said Poirot. He leaned back. "I think that that concludes the case. . . ."

There was silence in the room. They were all looking at the little man who sat there complacently stroking his mustache. On the inspector's face was perplexity, Dr. Stillingfleet was frowning, Cornworthy merely stared uncomprehendingly, Mrs. Farley gazed in blank astonishment, Joanna Farley looked eager.

Mrs. Farley broke the silence.

"I don't understand, M. Poirot." Her voice

was fretful. "The dream—"

"Yes," said Poirot. "That dream was very important."

Mrs. Farley shivered. She said:

"I've never believed in anything supernatural before—but now—to dream it night after night beforehand—"

"It's extraordinary," said Stillingfleet. "Extraordinary! If we hadn't got your word for it, Poirot, and if you hadn't had it straight from the horse's mouth—" he coughed in embarrassment, and readopting his professional manner, "I beg your pardon, Mrs. Farley. If Mr. Farley himself had not told that story—"

"Exactly," said Poirot. His eyes, which had been half-closed, opened suddenly. They were very green. *"If Benedict Farley hadn't told me—"*

He paused a minute, looking round at a circle of blank faces.

"There are certain things, you comprehend, that happened that evening which I was quite at a loss to explain. First, why make such a point of my bringing that letter with me?"

"Identification," suggested Cornworthy.

"No, no, my dear young man. Really that idea is too ridiculous. There must be some much more valid reason. For not only did Mr. Farley require to see that letter produced, but he definitely demanded that I should leave it behind me. And moreover even then he did not destroy it! It was found among his papers this afternoon. *Why did he keep it?*"

Joanna Farley's voice broke in. "He wanted, in case anything happened to him, that the facts of his strange dream should be made known."

Poirot nodded approvingly.

"You are astute, mademoiselle. That must be—that can only be—the point of the keeping of the letter. When Mr. Farley was dead, the story of that strange dream was to be told! That dream was very important. That dream, mademoiselle, was *vital!*

"I will come now," he went on, "to the second point. After hearing his story I ask Mr. Farley to show me the desk and the revolver. He seems about to get up to do so, then suddenly refuses. Why did he refuse?"

This time no one advanced an answer.

"I will put that question differently. *What was there in that next room that Mr. Farley did not want me to see?*"

There was still silence.

"Yes," said Poirot, "it is difficult, that. And yet there was some reason—some *urgent* reason why Mr. Farley received me in his secretary's room and refused point blank to take me into his own room. *There was something in that room he could not afford to have me see.*

"And now I come to the third inexplicable thing that happened on that evening. Mr. Farley, just as I was leaving, requested me to hand him the letter I had received. By inadvertence I handed him a communication from my laundress. He glanced at it and laid it down beside him. Just before I left the room I discovered my error—and rectified it! After that I left the house and—I admit it—I was completely at sea! The whole affair and especially that last incident seemed to me quite inexplicable."

He looked round from one to the other.

"You do not see?"

Stillingfleet said, "I don't really see how your laundress comes into it, Poirot."

"My laundress," said Poirot, "was very important. That miserable woman who ruins my collars, was, for the first time in her life, useful to somebody. Surely you see—it is so obvious. Mr. Farley glanced at that communication—*one glance* would have told him that it was the wrong letter— and yet he knew nothing. Why? *Because he could not see it properly!*"

Inspector Barnett said sharply, "Didn't he have his glasses on?"

Hercule Poirot smiled. "Yes," he said. "He had his glasses on. That is what makes it so very interesting."

He leaned forward.

"Mr. Farley's dream was very important. He dreamed, you see, that he committed suicide. And a little later on, he did commit suicide. That is to say he was alone in a room and was found there with a revolver by him, and no one entered or left the room at the time that he was shot. What does that mean? It means, does it not, that it *must* be suicide!"

"Yes," said Stillingfleet.

Hercule Poirot shook his head.

"On the contrary," he said. "It was murder. An unusual and a very cleverly planned murder."

Again he leaned forward, tapping the table, his eyes green and shining.

"Why did Mr. Farley not allow me to go into his own room that evening? What was there in there that I must not be allowed to see? I think, my friends, that there was—Benedict Farley himself!''

He smiled at the blank faces.

"Yes, yes, it is not nonsense what I say. Why could the Mr. Farley to whom I had been talking not realize the difference between two totally dissimilar letters? Because, *mes amis*, he was a man of *normal sight* wearing a pair of very powerful glasses. Those glasses would render a man of normal eyesight practically blind. Isn't that so, doctor?''

Stillingfleet murmured, "That's so—of course.''

"Why did I feel that in talking to Mr. Farley I was talking to a *mountebank*, to an actor playing a part? Because he *was* playing a part! Consider the setting. The dim room, the green shaded light turned blindingly away from the figure in the chair. What did I see—the famous patchwork dressing-gown, the beaked nose (faked with that useful substance, nose putty), the white crest of hair, the powerful lenses concealing the eyes. What evidence is there that Mr. Farley ever had a dream? Only the story I was told and the evidence of *Mrs. Farley*. What evidence is there that Benedict Farley kept a revolver in his desk? Again only the story told me and the word of Mrs. Farley. Two people carried this fraud through—Mrs. Farley and Hugo Cornworthy. Cornworthy wrote the letter to me, gave instructions to the butler, went out ostensibly to the cinema, but let himself in again immediately with a key, went to his room, made himself up, and played the part of Benedict Farley.

"And so we come to this afternoon. The opportunity for which Mr. Cornworthy has been waiting arrives. There are two witnesses on the landing to swear that no one goes in or out of Benedict Farley's room. Cornworthy waits until a particularly heavy batch of traffic is about to pass. Then he leans out of his window, and with the lazytongs which he has purloined from the desk next door he holds an object against the window of that room. Benedict Farley comes to the window. Cornworthy snatches back the tongs and as Farley leans out, and the lorries are passing outside, Cornworthy shoots him with the revolver that he has ready. There is a blank wall opposite, remember. There can be no witness of the crime. Cornworthy waits for over half an hour, then gathers up some papers, conceals the lazytongs and the revolver between them and goes out on to the landing and into the next room. He replaces the tongs on the desk, lays down the revolver after pressing the dead man's fingers on it, and hurries out with the news of Mr. Farley's 'suicide.'

"He arranges that the letter to me shall be found and that I shall arrive with my story—the story I heard *from Mr. Farley's own lips*—of his extraordinary 'dream'—the strange compulsion he felt to kill himself! A few credulous people will discuss the hypnotism theory—but the main result will be to confirm without a doubt that the actual hand that held the revolver was Benedict Farley's own."

Hercule Poirot's eyes went to the widow's face —the dismay—the ashy pallor—the blind fear.

"And in due course," he finished gently, "the happy ending would have been achieved. A quarter of a million and two hearts that beat as one. . . ."

John Stillingfleet, M.D., and Hercule Poirot walked along the side of Northway House. On their right was the towering wall of the factory. Above them, on their left, were the windows of Benedict Farley's and Hugo Cornworthy's rooms. Hercule Poirot stopped and picked up a small object—a black stuffed cat.

"*Voilà*," he said. "That is what Cornworthy held in the lazytongs against Farley's window. You remember, he hated cats? Naturally he rushed to the window."

"Why on earth didn't Cornworthy come out and pick it up after he'd dropped it?"

"How could he? To do so would have been definitely suspicious. After all, if this object where found what would anyone think—that some child had wandered round here and dropped it."

"Yes," said Stillingfleet with a sigh. "That's probably what the ordinary person *would* have thought. But not good old Hercule! D'you know, old horse, up to the very last minute I thought you were leading up to some subtle theory of highfalutin psychological 'suggested' murder? I bet those two thought so too! Nasty bit of goods, the Farley. Goodness, how she cracked! Cornworthy might have got away with it if she hadn't had hysterics and tried to spoil your beauty by going for you with her nails. I only got her off you just in time."

He paused a minute and then said:

"I rather like the girl. Grit, you know, and brains. I suppose I'd be thought to be a fortune hunter if I had a shot at her . . . ?"

"You are too late, my friend. There is already someone *sur le tapis*. Her father's death has opened the way to happiness."

"Take it all round, *she* had a pretty good motive for bumping off the unpleasant parent."

"Motive and opportunity are not enough," said Poirot. "There must also be the criminal temperament!"

"I wonder if you'll ever commit a crime, Poirot?" said Stillingfleet. "I bet you could get away with it all right. As a matter of fact, it would be *too* easy for you—I mean the thing would be off as definitely too unsporting."

"That," said Poirot, "is a typically English idea."

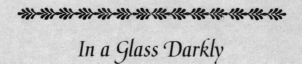

In a Glass Darkly

I've no explanation of this story. I've no theories about the why and wherefore of it. It's just a thing—that happened.

All the same, I sometimes wonder how things would have gone if I'd noticed at the time just that one essential detail that I never appreciated until so many years afterwards. If I *had* noticed it— well, I suppose the course of three lives would have been entirely altered. Somehow—that's a very frightening thought.

For the beginning of it all, I've got to go back to the summer of 1914—just before the war—when I went down to Badgeworthy with Neil Carslake. Neil was, I suppose, about my best friend. I'd known his brother Alan too, but not so well. Sylvia, their sister, I'd never met. She was two years younger than Alan and three years younger than Neil. Twice, while we were at school together, I'd been going to spend part of the holidays with Neil at Badgeworthy and twice something had intervened. So it came about that I was twenty-three when I first saw Neil and Alan's home.

We were to be quite a big party there. Neil's sister Sylvia had just got engaged to a fellow called Charles Crawley. He was, so Neil said, a good deal older than she was, but a thoroughly decent chap and quite reasonably well-off.

We arrived, I remember, about seven o'clock in the evening. Everyone had gone to his room to dress for dinner. Neil took me to mine. Badgeworthy was an attractive, rambling old house. It had been added to freely in the last three centuries and was full of little steps up and down, and unexpected staircases. It was the sort of house in which it's not too easy to find your way about. I remember Neil promised to come and fetch me on his way down to dinner. I was feeling a little shy at the prospect of meeting his people for the first time. I remember saying with a laugh that it was the kind of house where one expected to meet ghosts in the passages, and he said carelessly that he believed the place was said to be haunted but that none of them had ever seen anything, and he didn't even know what form the ghost was supposed to take.

Then he hurried away and I set to work to dive into my suitcases for my evening clothes. The Carslakes weren't well-off; they clung on to their old home, but there were no menservants to unpack for you or valet you.

Well, I'd just got to the stage of tying my tie. I was standing in front of the glass. I could see my own face and shoulders and behind them the wall of the room—a plain stretch of wall just broken in the middle by a door—and just as I had finally settled my tie I noticed that the door was opening.

I don't know why I didn't turn round—I think that would have been the natural thing to do; anyway, I didn't. I just watched the door swing slowly open—and as it swung I saw into the room beyond.

It was a bedroom—a larger room than mine—with two bedsteads in it, and suddenly I caught my breath.

For at the foot of one of those beds was a girl and round her neck were a pair of man's hands and the man was slowly forcing her backwards and squeezing her throat as he did so, so that the girl was being slowly suffocated.

There wasn't the least possibility of a mistake. What I saw was perfectly clear. What was being done was murder.

I could see the girl's face clearly, her vivid golden hair, the agonized terror of her beautiful face, slowly suffusing with blood. Of the man I could only see his back, his hands, and a scar that ran down the left side of his face towards his neck.

It's taken some time to tell, but in reality only a moment or two passed while I stared dumbfounded. Then I wheeled round to the rescue. . . .

And on the wall behind me, the wall reflected in the glass, there was only a large Victorian mahogany wardrobe. No open door—no scene of violence. I swung back to the mirror. The mirror reflected only the wardrobe. . . .

I passed my hands across my eyes. Then I sprang across the room and tried to pull forward the wardrobe and at that moment Neil entered by

the other door from the passage and asked me
what the hell I was trying to do.

He must have thought me slightly barmy as I
turned on him and demanded whether there was a
door behind the wardrobe. He said, yes, there was
a door, it led into the next room. I asked him who
was occupying the room and he said some people
called Oldham—a Major Oldham and his wife. I
asked him then if Mrs. Oldham had very fair hair
and when he replied dryly that she was dark I
began to realize that I was probably making a fool
of myself. I pulled myself together, made some
lame explanation and we went downstairs together. I told myself that I must have had some
kind of hallucination—and felt generally rather
ashamed and a bit of an ass.

And then—and then—Neil said, "My sister
Sylvia," and I was looking into the lovely face of
the girl I had just seen being suffocated to death
. . . and I was introduced to her fiancé, a tall, dark
man *with a scar down the left side of his face.*

Well—that's that. I'd like you to think and say
what you'd have done in my place. Here was the
girl—the identical girl—and here was the man I'd
seen throttling her—and they were to be married
in about a month's time. . . .

Had I—or had I not—had a prophetic vision of
the future? Would Sylvia and her husband come
down here to stay sometime in the future, and be
given that room (the best spare room) and would
that scene I'd witnessed take place in grim reality?

What was I to do about it? *Could* I do anything? Would anyone—Neil—or the girl herself—
would they believe me?

I turned the whole business over and over in my mind the week I was down there. To speak or not to speak? And almost at once another complication set in. You see, I fell in love with Sylvia Carslake the first moment I saw her. . . . I wanted her more than anything on earth. . . . And in a way that tied my hands.

And yet, if I didn't say anything, Sylvia would marry Charles Crawley and Crawley would kill her. . . .

And so, the day before I left, I blurted it all out to her. I said I expected she'd think me touched in the intellect or something but I swore solemnly that I'd seen the thing just as I told it to her and that I felt if she was determined to marry Crawley, I ought to tell her my strange experience.

She listened very quietly. There was something in her eyes I didn't understand. She wasn't angry at all. When I'd finished, she just thanked me gravely. I kept repeating like an idiot, "I *did* see it. I really did see it," and she said, "I'm sure you did if you say so. I believe you."

Well, the upshot was that I went off not knowing whether I'd done right or been a fool, and a week later Sylvia broke off her engagement to Charles Crawley.

After that the war happened, and there wasn't much leisure for thinking of anything else. Once or twice when I was on leave, I came across Sylvia, but as far as possible I avoided her.

I loved her and wanted her just as badly as ever, but I felt, somehow, that it wouldn't be playing the game. It was owing to me that she'd broken off her engagement to Crawley, and I kept saying to myself that I could only justify the action I had taken by making my attitude a purely disinterested one.

Then, in 1916, Neil was killed and it fell to me to tell Sylvia about his last moments. We couldn't remain on a formal footing after that. Sylvia had adored Neil and he had been my best friend. She was sweet—adorably sweet in her grief. I just managed to hold my tongue and went out again praying that a bullet might end the whole miserable business. Life without Sylvia wasn't worth living.

But there was no bullet with my name on it. One nearly got me below the right ear and one was deflected by a cigarette case in my pocket, but I came through unscathed. Charles Crawley was killed in action at the beginning of 1918.

Somehow—that made a difference. I came home in the autumn of 1918 just before the Armistice and I went straight to Sylvia and told her that I loved her. I hadn't much hope that she'd care for me straight away, and you could have knocked me down with a feather when she asked me why I hadn't told her sooner. I stammered out something about Crawley and she said, "But why did you think I broke it off with him?" And then she told me that she'd fallen in love with me just as I'd done with her—from the very first minute.

I said I thought she'd broken off her engagement because of the story I told her and she laughed scornfully and said that if you loved a man you wouldn't be as cowardly as that, and we went over that old vision of mine again and agreed that it was queer, but nothing more.

Well, there's nothing much to tell for some time

after that. Sylvia and I were married and we were happy. But I realized, as soon as she was really mine, that I wasn't cut out for the best kind of husband. I loved Sylvia devotedly, but I was jealous, absurdly jealous of anyone she so much as smiled at. It amused her at first. I think she even rather liked it. It proved, at least, how devoted I was.

As for me, I realized quite fully and unmistakably that I was not only making a fool of myself, but that I was endangering all the peace and happiness of our life together. I knew, I say, but I couldn't change. Every time Sylvia got a letter she didn't show to me I wondered who it was from. If she laughed and talked with any man, I found myself getting sulky and watchful.

At first, as I say, Sylvia laughed at me. She thought it a huge joke. Then she didn't think the joke so funny. Finally she didn't think it a joke at all—

And slowly, she began to draw away from me. Not in any physical sense, but she withdrew her secret mind from me. I no longer knew what her thoughts were. She was kind—but sadly, as though from a long distance.

Little by little I realized that she no longer loved me. Her love had died and it was I who had killed it. . . .

The next step was inevitable. I found myself waiting for it—dreading it. . . .

Then Derek Wainwright came into our lives. He had everything that I hadn't. He had brains and a witty tongue. He was good-looking, too, and—I'm forced to admit it—a thoroughly good chap. As soon as I saw him I said to myself, "This is just the man for Sylvia. . . ."

She fought against it. I know she struggled . . . but I gave her no help. I couldn't. I was entrenched in my gloomy, sullen reserve. I was suffering like hell—and I couldn't stretch out a finger to save myself. I didn't help her. I made things worse. I let loose at her one day—a string of savage, unwarranted abuse. I was nearly mad with jealousy and misery. The things I said were cruel and untrue and I knew while I was saying them how cruel and how untrue they were. And yet I took a savage pleasure in saying them. . . .

I remember how Sylvia flushed and shrank. . . .

I drove her to the edge of endurance.

I remember she said, "This can't go on. . . ."

When I came home that night the house was empty—empty. There was a note—quite in the traditional fashion.

In it she said that she was leaving me—for good. She was going down to Badgeworthy for a day or two. After that she was going to the one person who loved her and needed her. I was to take that as final.

I suppose that up to then I hadn't really believed my own suspicions. This confirmation in black and white of my worst fears sent me raving mad. I went down to Badgeworthy after her as fast as the car would take me.

She had just changed her frock for dinner, I remember, when I burst into the room. I can see her face—startled—beautiful—afraid.

I said, "No one but me shall ever have you. No one."

And I caught her throat in my hands and gripped it and bent her backwards.

And suddenly I saw our reflection in the mirror. Sylvia choking and myself strangling her, and the scar on my cheek where the bullet grazed it under the right ear.

No—I didn't kill her. That sudden revelation paralyzed me and I loosened my grasp and let her slip onto the floor. . . .

And then I broke down—and she comforted me. . . . Yes, she comforted me.

I told her everything and she told me that by the phrase "the one person who loved and needed her" she had meant her brother Alan. . . . We saw into each other's hearts that night, and I don't think, from that moment, that we ever drifted away from each other again. . . .

It's a sobering thought to go through life with —that, but for the grace of God and a mirror, one might be a murderer. . . .

One thing did die that night—the devil of jealousy that had possessed me so long. . . .

But I wonder sometimes—suppose I hadn't made that initial mistake—the scar on the *left* cheek—when really it was the *right*—reversed by the mirror. . . . Should I have been so sure the man was Charles Crawley? Would I have warned Sylvia? Would she be married to me—or to him?

Or are the past and the future all one?

I'm a simple fellow—and I can't pretend to understand these things—but I saw what I saw— and because of what I saw, Sylvia and I are together—in the old-fashioned words—till death do us part. And perhaps beyond. . . .

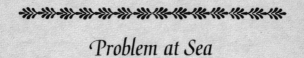

Problem at Sea

"Colonel Clapperton!" said General Forbes.

He said it with an effect midway between a snort and a sniff.

Miss Ellie Henderson leaned forward, a strand of her soft gray hair blowing across her face. Her eyes, dark and snapping, gleamed with a wicked pleasure.

"Such a *soldierly*-looking man!" she said with malicious intent, and smoothed back the lock of hair to await the result.

"Soldierly!" exploded General Forbes. He tugged at his military mustache and his face became bright red.

"In the Guards, wasn't he?" murmured Miss Henderson, completing her work.

"Guards? Guards? Pack of nonsense. Fellow was on the music hall stage! Fact! Joined up and was out in France counting tins of plum and apple. Huns dropped a stray bomb and he went home with a flesh wound in the arm. Somehow or other got into Lady Carrington's hospital.''

"So that's how they met.''

"Fact! Fellow played the wounded hero. Lady Carrington had no sense and oceans of money. Old Carrington had been in munitions. She'd been a widow only six months. This fellow snaps her up in no time. She wangled him a job at the War Office. *Colonel* Clapperton! Pah!'' he snorted.

"And before the war he was on the music hall stage,'' mused Miss Henderson, trying to reconcile the distinguished gray-haired Colonel Clapperton with a red-nosed comedian singing mirth-provoking songs.

"Fact!'' said General Forbes. "Heard it from old Bassington-ffrench. And he heard it from old Badger Cotterill who'd got it from Snooks Parker.''

Miss Henderson nodded brightly. "That does seem to settle it!'' she said.

A fleeting smile showed for a minute on the face of a small man sitting near them. Miss Henderson noticed the smile. She was observant. It had shown appreciation of the irony underlying her last remark—irony which the General never for a moment suspected.

The General himself did not notice the smiles. He glanced at his watch, rose and remarked: "Exercise. Got to keep oneself fit on a boat,'' and passed out through the open door onto the deck.

Miss Henderson glanced at the man who had smiled. It was a well-bred glance indicating that she was ready to enter into conversation with a fellow traveler.

"He is energetic—yes?" said the little man.

"He goes round the deck forty-eight times exactly," said Miss Henderson. "What an old gossip! And they say *we* are the scandal-loving sex."

"What an impoliteness!"

"Frenchmen are always polite," said Miss Henderson—there was the nuance of a question in her voice.

The little man responded promptly. "Belgian, Mademoiselle."

"Oh! Belgian."

"Hercule Poirot. At your service."

The name aroused some memory. Surely she had heard it before—? "Are you enjoying this trip, M. Poirot?"

"Frankly, no. It was an imbecility to allow myself to be persuaded to come. I detest *la mer*. Never does it remain tranquil—no, not for a little minute."

"Well, you admit it's quite calm now."

M. Poirot admitted this grudgingly. "*À ce moment*, yes. That is why I revive. I once more interest myself in what passes around me—your very adept handling of the General Forbes, for instance."

"You mean—" Miss Henderson paused.

Hercule Poirot bowed. "Your methods of extracting the scandalous matter. Admirable!"

Miss Henderson laughed in an unashamed manner. "That touch about the Guards? I knew that would bring the old boy up spluttering and gasping." She leaned forward confidentially. "I admit I *like* scandal—the more ill-natured, the better!"

Poirot looked thoughtfully at her—her slim

well-preserved figure, her keen dark eyes, her gray hair; a woman of forty-five who was content to look her age.

Ellie said abruptly: "I have it! Aren't you the great detective?"

Poirot bowed. "You are too amiable, Mademoiselle." But he made no disclaimer.

"How thrilling," said Miss Henderson. "Are you 'hot on the trail' as they say in books? Have we a criminal secretly in our midst? Or am I being indiscreet?"

"Not at all. Not at all. It pains me to disappoint your expectations, but I am simply here, like everyone else, to amuse myself."

He said it in such a gloomy voice that Miss Henderson laughed.

"Oh! Well, you will be able to get ashore tomorrow at Alexandria. You have been to Egypt before?"

"Never, Mademoiselle."

Miss Henderson rose somewhat abruptly.

"I think I shall join the General on his constitutional," she announced.

Poirot sprang politely to his feet.

She gave him a little nod and passed out onto the deck.

A faint puzzled look showed for a moment in Poirot's eyes then, a little smile creasing his lips, he rose, put his head through the door and glanced down the deck. Miss Henderson was leaning against the rail talking to a tall, soldierly-looking man.

Poirot's smile deepened. He drew himself back into the smoking-room with the same exaggerated care with which a tortoise withdraws itself into its shell. For the moment he had the smoking-room to himself, though he rightly conjectured that that would not last long.

It did not. Mrs. Clapperton, her carefully waved platinum head protected with a net, her massaged and dieted form dressed in a smart sports suit, came through the door from the bar with the purposeful air of a woman who has always been able to pay top price for anything she needed.

She said: "John—? Oh! Good-morning, M. Poirot—have you seen John?"

"He's on the starboard deck, Madame. Shall I—?"

She arrested him with a gesture. "I'll sit here a minute." She sat down in a regal fashion in the chair opposite him. From the distance she had looked a possible twenty-eight. Now, in spite of her exquisitely made-up face, her delicately plucked eyebrows, she looked not her actual forty-nine years, but a possible fifty-five. Her eyes were a hard pale blue with tiny pupils.

"I was sorry not to have seen you at dinner last night," she said. "It was just a shade choppy, of course—"

"Précisément," said Poirot with feeling.

"Luckily, I am an excellent sailor," said Mrs. Clapperton. "I say luckily, because, with my weak heart, seasickness would probably be the death of me."

"You have the weak heart, Madame?"

"Yes, I have to be *most* careful. I must *not* overtire myself! *All* the specialists say so!" Mrs. Clapperton had embarked on the—to her—ever-fascinating topic of her health. "John, poor darling, wears himself out trying to prevent me from doing too much. I live so intensely, if you know what I mean, M. Poirot?''

"Yes, yes."

"He always says to me: 'Try to be more of a vegetable, Adeline.' But I can't. Life was meant to be *lived*, I feel. As a matter of fact I wore myself out as a girl in the war. My hospital—you've heard of my hospital? Of course I had nurses and matrons and all that—but *I* actually ran it.'' She sighed.

"Your vitality is marvelous, dear lady," said Poirot, with the slightly mechanical air of one responding to his cue.

Mrs. Clapperton gave a girlish laugh.

"Everyone tells me how young I am! It's absurd. I never try to pretend I'm a day less than forty-three," she continued with slightly mendacious candor, "but a lot of people find it hard to believe. 'You're so *alive*, Adeline,' they say to me. But really, M. Poirot, what would one *be* if one wasn't alive?''

"Dead," said Poirot.

Mrs. Clapperton frowned. The reply was not to her liking. The man, she decided, was trying to be funny. She got up and said coldly: "I must find John."

As she stepped through the door she dropped her handbag. It opened and the contents flew far and wide. Poirot rushed gallantly to the rescue. It was some few minutes before the lipsticks, vanity boxes, cigarette case and lighter and other odds and ends were collected. Mrs. Clapperton thanked him politely, then she swept down the deck and said, "John—"

Colonel Clapperton was still deep in conversation with Miss Henderson. He swung round and came quickly to meet his wife. He bent over her protectively. Her deck chair—was it in the right place? Wouldn't it be better—? His manner was courteous—full of gentle consideration. Clearly an adored wife spoilt by an adoring husband.

Miss Ellie Henderson looked out at the horizon as though something about it rather disgusted her.

Standing in the smoking-room door, Poirot looked on.

A hoarse quavering voice behind him said:

"I'd take a hatchet to that woman if I were her husband." The old gentleman known disrespectfully among the Younger Set on board as the Grandfather of All the Tea Planters, had just shuffled in. "Boy!" he called. "Get me a whisky peg."

Poirot stooped to retrieve a torn scrap of notepaper, an overlooked item from the contents of Mrs. Clapperton's bag. Part of a prescription, he noted, containing digitalin. He put it in his pocket, meaning to restore it to Mrs. Clapperton later.

"Yes," went on the aged passenger. Poisonous woman. I remember a woman like that in Poona. In '87 that was."

"Did anyone take a hatchet to her?" inquired Poirot.

The old gentleman shook his head sadly.

"Worried her husband into his grave within the year. Clapperton ought to assert himself. Gives his wife her head too much."

"She holds the purse strings," said Poirot gravely.

"Ha ha!" chuckled the old gentleman. "You've put the matter in a nutshell. Holds the purse strings. Ha ha!"

Two girls burst into the smoking-room. One had a round face with freckles and dark hair streaming out in a windswept confusion, the other had freckles and curly chestnut hair.

"A rescue—a rescue!" cried Kitty Mooney. "Pam and I are going to rescue Colonel Clapperton."

"From his wife," gasped Pamela Cregan.

"We think he's a *pet*. . . ."

"And she's just awful—she won't let him do *anything*," the two girls exclaimed.

"And if he isn't with her, he's usually grabbed by the Henderson woman. . . ."

"Who's quite nice. But terribly *old*. . . ."

They ran out, gasping in between giggles:

"A rescue—a rescue . . ."

That the rescue of Colonel Clapperton was no isolated sally, but a fixed project was made clear that same evening when the eighteen-year-old Pam Cregan came up to Hercule Poirot, and murmured: "Watch us, M. Poirot. He's going to be cut out from under her nose and taken to walk in the moonlight on the boat deck."

It was just at that moment that Colonel Clapperton was saying: "I grant you the price of a Rolls Royce. But it's practically good for a lifetime. Now my car—"

"*My* car, I think, John." Mrs. Clapperton's voice was shrill and penetrating.

He showed no annoyance at her ungraciousness. Either he was used to it by this time, or else—

"Or else?" thought Poirot and let himself speculate.

"Certainly, my dear, *your* car," Clapperton bowed to his wife and finished what he had been saying, perfectly unruffled.

"Voilà ce qu'on appelle le pukka sahib," thought Poirot. "But the General Forbes says that Clapperton is no gentleman at all. I wonder now."

There was a suggestion of bridge. Mrs. Clapperton, General Forbes and a hawk-eyed couple sat down to it. Miss Henderson had excused herself and gone out on deck.

"What about your husband?" asked General Forbes, hesitating.

"John won't play," said Mrs. Clapperton. "Most tiresome of him."

The four bridge players began shuffling the cards.

Pam and Kitty advanced on Colonel Clapperton. Each one took an arm.

"You're coming with us!" said Pam. "To the boat deck. There's a moon."

"Don't be foolish, John," said Mrs. Clapperton. "You'll catch a chill."

"Not with us, he won't," said Kitty. "We're hot stuff!"

He went with them, laughing.

Poirot noticed that Mrs. Clapperton said No Bid to her initial bid of Two Clubs.

He strolled out onto the promenade deck. Miss Henderson was standing by the rail. She looked round expectantly as he came to stand beside her and he saw the drop in her expression.

They chatted for a while. Then presently as he fell silent she asked: "What are you thinking about?"

Poirot replied: "I am wondering about my knowledge of English. Mrs. Clapperton said: 'John won't play bridge.' Is not 'can't play' the usual term?"

"She takes it as a personal insult that he doesn't, I suppose," said Ellie drily. "The man was a fool ever to have married her."

In the darkness Poirot smiled. "You don't think it's just possible that the marriage may be a success?" he asked diffidently.

"With a woman like that?"

Poirot shrugged his shoulders. "Many odious women have devoted husbands. An enigma of Nature. You will admit that nothing she says or does appears to gall him."

Miss Henderson was considering her reply when Mrs. Clapperton's voice floated out through the smoking-room window.

"No—I don't think I will play another rubber. So stuffy. I think I'll go up and get some air on the boat deck."

"Good-night," said Miss Henderson. "I'm going to bed." She disappeared abruptly.

Poirot strolled forward to the lounge—deserted save for Colonel Clapperton and the two girls. He was doing card tricks for them, and noting the dexterity of his shuffling and handling of the cards, Poirot remembered the General's story of a career on the music hall stage.

"I see you enjoy the cards even though you do

not play bridge," he remarked.

"I've my reasons for not playing bridge," said Clapperton, his charming smile breaking out. "I'll show you. We'll play one hand."

He dealt the cards rapidly. "Pick up your hands. Well, what about it?" He laughed at the bewildered expression on Kitty's face. He laid down his hand and the others followed suit. Kitty held the entire club suit, M. Poirot the hearts, Pam the diamonds and Colonel Clapperton the spades.

"You see?" he said. "A man who can deal his partner and his adversaries any hand he pleases had better stand aloof from a friendly game! If the luck goes too much his way, ill-natured things might be said."

"Oh!" gasped Kitty. "How *could* you do that? It all looked perfectly ordinary."

"The quickness of the hand deceives the eye," said Poirot sententiously—and caught the sudden change in the Colonel's expression.

It was as though he realized that he had been off his guard for a moment or two.

Poirot smiled. The conjuror had shown himself through the mask of the *pukka sahib*.

The ship reached Alexandria at dawn the following morning.

As Poirot came up from breakfast he found the two girls all ready to go on shore. They were talking to Colonel Clapperton.

"We ought to get off now," urged Kitty. "The passport people will be going off the ship presently. You'll come with us, won't you? You wouldn't let us go ashore all by ourselves? Awful things might happen to us.''

"I certainly don't think you ought to go by yourselves,'' said Clapperton, smiling. "But I'm not sure my wife feels up to it.''

"That's too bad,'' said Pam. "But she can have a nice long rest.''

Colonel Clapperton looked a little irresolute. Evidently the desire to play truant was strong upon him. He noticed Poirot.

"Hullo, M. Poirot—you going ashore?''

"No, I think not,'' M. Poirot replied.

"I'll—I'll—just have a word with Adeline,'' decided Colonel Clapperton.

"We'll come with you,'' said Pam. She flashed a wink at Poirot. "Perhaps we can persuade her to come too,'' she added gravely.

Colonel Clapperton seemed to welcome this suggestion. He looked decidedly relieved.

"Come along then, the pair of you,'' he said lightly. They all three went along the passage of B deck together.

Poirot, whose cabin was just opposite the Clappertons, followed them out of curiosity.

Colonel Clapperton rapped a little nervously at the cabin door.

"Adeline, my dear, are you up?''

The sleepy voice of Mrs. Clapperton from within replied: "Oh, bother—what is it?''

"It's John. What about going ashore?''

"Certainly not.'' The voice was shrill and decisive. "I've had a very bad night. I shall stay in bed most of the day.''

Pam nipped in quickly, "Oh, Mrs. Clapperton,

I'm so sorry. We did so want you to come with us. Are you sure you're not up to it?"

"I'm quite certain." Mrs. Clapperton's voice sounded even shriller.

The Colonel was turning the door-handle without result.

"What is it, John? The door's locked. I don't want to be disturbed by the stewards."

"Sorry, my dear, sorry. Just wanted my Baedeker."

"Well, you can't have it," snapped Mrs. Clapperton. "I'm not going to get out of bed. Do go away, John, and let me have a little peace."

"Certainly, certainly, my dear." The Colonel backed away from the door. Pam and Kitty closed in on him.

"Let's start at once. Thank goodness your hat's on your head. Oh! gracious—your passport isn't in the cabin, is it?"

"As a matter of fact it's in my pocket—" began the Colonel.

Kitty squeezed his arm. "Glory be!" she exclaimed. "Now, come on."

Leaning over the rail, Poirot watched the three of them leave the ship. He heard a faint intake of breath beside him and turned his head to see Miss Henderson. Her eyes were fastened on the three retreating figures.

"So they've gone ashore," she said flatly.

"Yes. Are you going?"

She had a shade hat, he noticed, and a smart bag and shoes. There was a shore-going appearance about her. Nevertheless, after the most infinitesimal of pauses, she shook her head.

"No," she said. "I think I'll stay on board. I have a lot of letters to write."

She turned and left him.

Puffing after his morning tour of forty-eight rounds of the deck, General Forbes took her place. "Aha!" he exclaimed as his eyes noted the retreating figures of the Colonel and the two girls. "So *that's* the game! Where's the Madam?"

Poirot explained that Mrs. Clapperton was having a quiet day in bed.

"Don't you believe it!" The old warrior closed one knowing eye. "She'll be up for tiffin—and if the poor devil's found to be absent without leave, there'll be ructions."

But the General's prognostications were not fulfilled. Mrs. Clapperton did not appear at lunch and by the time the Colonel and his attendant damsels returned to the ship at four o'clock, she had not shown herself.

Poirot was in his cabin and heard the husband's slightly guilty knock on his cabin door. Heard the knock repeated, the cabin door tried, and finally heard the Colonel's call to a steward.

"Look here, I can't get an answer. Have you a key?"

Poirot rose quickly from his bunk and came out into the passage.

The news went like wildfire round the ship. With horrified incredulity people heard that Mrs. Clapperton had been found dead in her bunk—a native dagger driven through her heart. A string of amber beads was found on the floor of her cabin.

Rumor succeeded rumor. All bead sellers who

had been allowed on board that day were being
rounded up and questioned! A large sum in cash
had disappeared from a drawer in the cabin! The
notes had been traced! They had not been traced!
Jewelry worth a fortune had been taken! No
jewelry had been taken at all! A steward had been
arrested and had confessed to the murder!

"What is the truth of it all?" demanded Miss
Ellie Henderson, waylaying Poirot. Her face was
pale and troubled.

"My dear lady, how should I know?"

"Of course you know," said Miss Henderson.

It was late in the evening. Most people had
retired to their cabins. Miss Henderson led Poirot
to a couple of deck chairs on the sheltered side of
the ship. "Now tell me," she commanded.

Poirot surveyed her thoughtfully. "It's an interesting case," he said.

"Is it true that she had some very valuable
jewelry stolen?"

Poirot shook his head. "No. No jewelry was
taken. A small amount of loose cash that was in a
drawer has disappeared, though."

"I'll never feel safe on a ship again," said Miss
Henderson with a shiver. "Any clue as to which of
those coffee-colored brutes did it?"

"No," said Hercule Poirot. "The whole thing is
rather—strange."

"What do you mean?" asked Ellie sharply.

Poirot spread out his hands. "*Eh bien*—take
the facts. Mrs. Clapperton had been dead at least
five hours when she was found. Some money had
disappeared. A string of beads was on the floor by
her bed. The door was locked and the key was

missing. The window—*window*, not port-hole—gives on the deck and was open."

"Well?" asked the woman impatiently.

"Do you not think it is curious for a murder to be committed under those particular circumstances? Remember that the postcard sellers, money changers and bead sellers who are allowed on board are all well known to the police."

"The stewards usually lock your cabin, all the same," Ellie pointed out.

"Yes, to prevent any chance of petty pilfering. But this—was murder."

"What exactly are you thinking of, M. Poirot?" Her voice sounded a little breathless.

"I am thinking of the *locked door*."

Miss Henderson considered this. "I don't see anything in that. The man left by the door, locked it and took the key with him so as to avoid having the murder discovered too soon. Quite intelligent of him, for it wasn't discovered until four o'clock in the afternoon."

"No, no, Mademoiselle, you don't appreciate the point I'm trying to make. I'm not worried as to how he got *out*, but as to how he got *in*."

"The window of course."

"*C'est possible*. But it would be a very narrow fit—and there were people passing up and down the deck all the time, remember."

"Then through the door," said Miss Henderson impatiently.

"But you forget, Mademoiselle. *Mrs. Clapperton had locked the door on the inside*. She had done so before Colonel Clapperton left the boat this morning. He actually tried it—so we *know* that is so."

"Nonsense. It probably stuck—or he didn't turn the handle properly."

"But it does not rest on his word. We actually heard *Mrs. Clapperton herself say so*."

"We?"

"Miss Mooney, Miss Cregan, Colonel Clapperton and myself."

Ellie Henderson tapped a neatly shod foot. She did not speak for a moment or two. Then she said in a slightly irritable tone:

"Well—what exactly do you deduce from that? If Mrs. Clapperton could lock the door she could unlock it too, I suppose."

"Precisely, precisely." Poirot turned a beaming face upon her. "And you see where that leads us. *Mrs. Clapperton unlocked the door and let the murderer in*. Now would she be likely to do that *for a* bead seller?"

Ellie objected: "She might not have known who it was. He may have knocked—she got up and opened the door—and he forced his way in and killed her."

Poirot shook his head. "*Au contraire.* She was lying peacefully in bed when she was stabbed."

Miss Henderson stared at him. "What's your idea?" she asked abruptly.

Poirot smiled. "Well, it looks, does it not, as though she *knew* the person she admitted. . . ."

"You mean," said Miss Henderson and her voice sounded a little harsh, "*that the murderer is a passenger on the ship?*"

Poirot nodded. "It seems indicated."

"And the string of beads left on the floor was a blind?"

"Precisely."

"The theft of the money also?"

"Exactly."

There was a pause, then Miss Henderson said slowly: "I thought Mrs. Clapperton a very unpleasant woman and I don't think anyone on board really liked her—but there wasn't anyone who had any reason to kill her."

"Except her husband, perhaps," said Poirot.

"You don't really think—" She stopped.

"It is the opinion of every person on this ship that Colonel Clapperton would have been quite justified in 'taking a hatchet to her.' That was, I think, the expression used."

Ellie Henderson looked at him—waiting.

"But I am bound to say," went on Poirot, "that I myself have not noted any signs of exasperation on the good Colonel's part. Also, what is more important, he had an alibi. He was with those two girls all day and did not return to the ship till four o'clock. By then, Mrs. Clapperton had been dead many hours."

There was another minute of silence. Ellie Henderson said softly: "But you still think—a passenger on the ship?"

Poirot bowed his head.

Ellie Henderson laughed suddenly—a reckless defiant laugh. "Your theory may be difficult to prove, M. Poirot. There are a good many passengers on this ship."

Poirot bowed to her. "I will use a phrase from one of your detective story writers. 'I have my methods, Watson.' "

The following evening, at dinner, every passenger found a typewritten slip by his plate requesting him to be in the main lounge at 8:30. When the company were assembled, the Captain stepped onto the raised platform where the orchestra usually played and addressed them.

"Ladies and Gentlemen, you all know of the tragedy which took place yesterday. I am sure you all wish to co-operate in bringing the perpetrator of that foul crime to justice." He paused and cleared his throat. "We have on board with us M. Hercule Poirot who is probably known to you all as a man who has had wide experience in—er— such matters. I hope you will listen carefully to what he has to say."

It was at this minute that Colonel Clapperton who had not been at dinner came in and sat down next to General Forbes. He looked like a man bewildered by sorrow—not at all like a man conscious of great relief. Either he was a very good actor or else he had been genuinely fond of his disagreeable wife.

"M. Hercule Poirot," said the Captain and stepped down. Poirot took his place. He looked comically self-important as he beamed on his audience.

"Messieurs, Mesdames," he began. "It is most kind of you to be so indulgent as to listen to me. *M. le Capitaine* has told you that I have had a certain experience in these matters. I have, it is true, a little idea of my own about how to get to the bottom of this particular case." He made a sign and a steward pushed forward and passed up to him a bulky, shapeless object wrapped in a sheet.

"What I am about to do may surprise you a

little," Poirot warned them. "It may occur to you that I am eccentric, perhaps mad. Nevertheless I assure you that behind my madness there is—as you English say—a method."

His eyes met those of Miss Henderson for just a minute. He began unwrapping the bulky object.

"I have here, *Messieurs* and *Mesdames*, an important witness to the truth of who killed Mrs. Clapperton." With a deft hand he whisked away the last enveloping cloth, and the object it concealed was revealed—an almost life-sized wooden doll, dressed in a velvet suit and lace collar.

"Now, Arthur," said Poirot and his voice changed subtly—it was no longer foreign—it had instead a confident English, a slightly Cockney inflection. "Can you tell me—I repeat—can you tell me—anything at all about the death of Mrs. Clapperton?"

The doll's neck oscillated a little, its wooden lower jaw dropped and wavered and a shrill high-pitched woman's voice spoke:

"What is it, John? The door's locked. I don't want to be disturbed by the stewards. . . ."

There was a cry—an overturned chair—a man stood swaying, his hand to his throat—trying to speak—trying . . . Then suddenly, his figure seemed to crumple up. He pitched headlong.

It was Colonel Clapperton.

Poirot and the ship's doctor rose from their knees by the prostrate figure.

"All over, I'm afraid. Heart," said the doctor briefly.

Poirot nodded. "The shock of having his trick seen through," he said.

He turned to General Forbes. "It was you, General, who gave me a valuable hint with your mention of the music hall stage. I puzzle—I think—and then it comes to me. Supposing that before the war Clapperton was a *ventriloquist*. In that case, it would be perfectly possible for three people to hear Mrs. Clapperton speak from inside her cabin *when she was already dead*. . . ."

Ellie Henderson was beside him. Her eyes were dark and full of pain. "Did you know his heart was weak?" she asked.

"I guessed it. . . . Mrs. Clapperton talked of her own heart being affected, but she struck me as the type of woman who likes to be thought ill. Then I picked up a torn prescription with a very strong dose of digitalin in it. Digitalin is a heart medicine but it couldn't be Mrs. Clapperton's because digitalin dilates the pupils of the eyes. I had never noticed such a phenomenon with her—but when I looked at his eyes I saw the signs at once."

Ellie murmured: "So you thought—it might end—this way?"

"The best way, don't you think, Mademoiselle?" he said gently.

He saw the tears rise in her eyes. She said: "You've known. You've known all along. . . . That I cared. . . . But he didn't do it for *me*. . . . It was those girls—youth—it made him feel his slavery. He wanted to be free before it was too late. . . . Yes, I'm sure that's how it was. . . . When did you guess—that it was he?"

"His self-control was too perfect," said Poirot simply. "No matter how galling his wife's conduct, it never seemed to touch him. That meant either that he was so used to it that it no longer stung him, or else—*eh bien*—I decided on the latter alternative. . . . And I was right. . . .

"And then there was his insistence on his conjuring ability—the evening before the crime. He pretended to give himself away. But a man like Clapperton doesn't give himself away. There must be a reason. So long as people thought he had been a *conjuror* they weren't likely to think of his having been a *ventriloquist*."

"And the voice we heard—Mrs. Clapperton's voice?"

"One of the stewardesses had a voice not unlike hers. I induced her to hide behind the stage and taught her the words to say."

"It was a trick—a cruel trick," cried out Ellie.

"I do not approve of murder," said Hercule Poirot.

AGATHA CHRISTIE

Mystery's #1 Bestseller!

"One of the most imaginative and fertile plot creators of all time!"

—Ellery Queen

Agatha Christie is the world's most brilliant and most famous mystery writer, as well as one of the greatest storytellers of all time. And now, Berkley presents a mystery lover's paradise—35 classics from this unsurpassed Queen of Mystery.

"Agatha Christie...what more could a mystery addict desire?"

—The New York Times

Available Now

NGAIO MARSH

BESTSELLING PAPERBACKS BY A "GRAND MASTER" OF THE MYSTERY WRITERS OF AMERICA.

NGAIO MARSH

____	07507-8 NIGHT AT THE VULCAN	$2.95
____	06822-5 OVERTURE TO DEATH	$2.50
____	07505-1 PHOTO FINISH	$2.95
____	07504-3 WHEN IN ROME	$2.95
____	06014-3 COLOUR SCHEME	$2.50
____	07440-3 DEAD WATER	$2.95
____	06700-8 DEATH AT THE BAR	$2.50
____	06007-0 FALSE SCENT	$2.50
____	05967-6 THE NURSING HOME MURDER	$2.50
____	06179-4 SPINSTERS IN JEOPARDY	$2.50
____	06015-1 TIED UP IN TINSEL	$2.50
____	06012-7 VINTAGE MURDER	$2.50
____	06016-X A WREATH FOR RIVERA	$2.50
____	06497-1 SCALES OF JUSTICE	$2.50

Prices may be slightly higher in Canada.
